COMING BACK

MARCIA MULLER

GRAND CENTRAL
PUBLISHING

NEW YORK   BOSTON

30491 6305

Copyright © 2010 by Pronzini-Muller Family Trust

Grand Central Publishing
Hachette Book Group
237 Park Avenue
New York, NY 10017

www.HachetteBookGroup.com

Printed in the United States of America

First Edition: October 2010
10 9 8 7 6 5 4 3 2 1

Grand Central Publishing is a division of Hachette Book Group, Inc.
The Grand Central Publishing name and logo is a trademark of Hachette Book Group, Inc.

Library of Congress Cataloging-in-Publication Data

Muller, Marcia.
  Coming back / Marcia Muller.
    p. cm.
  ISBN 978-0-446-58106-6
  1. McCone, Sharon (Fictitious character)—Fiction. 2. Women private investigators—Fiction. I. Title.
  PS3563.U397C66 2010
  813'.54—dc22
                                                        2009046973

For all those who came back
And those who waited for them

*As always, thanks to Bill, my inspiration and first editor,
and to Sharon McCone, who sits on my shoulder
and tells me what to write.*

TRYING DESPERATELY

"What do you know about it?"
he sneered. "You've never
worked." He added, "Unless
you're going to count
those four months you worked
as a telephone solicitor."
My eyes narrowed. "Three,"
I said. "It was only for
three months." I added,
"Work is what you do
when everything depends
on what you do." Calmly,
I listed my qualifications:
"Nine weeks in a coma,
seven months in hospitals,
five operations,
two crushed knees,
brain damage that resulted
in a stroke, seven pelvic
fractures—and I still
carried a baby to term."
Quietly, I added, "I work more
in an hour than you do
in a day. Trying desperately
to stay on my feet. Trying
desperately not to snarl
my words. Trying desperately
to be normal."

—Kit Knight

JULY–JANUARY

SHARON McCONE

*C*oming back was the hardest thing I've ever had to do.

First the speech: trying to make coherent words out of the gibberish that spewed from my lips. Like learning English as a second language, only as if I had no first.

"Mescatal," I said to Phoebe Williams, my speech therapist at the Brandt Neurological Institute; I'd been a patient there since I was shot in the head in early July by an intruder at Pier 24½. Phoebe had asked me what abilities I'd normally lacked before I spent two weeks in a coma.

In spite of the scrambled word, she knew what I meant. "Mus-i-cal." She accented the first syllable, using a long U slowly, showing me how she moved her mouth and tongue.

"Musicattle." At least the first two syllables were right.

"Mus-i-cal."

"Mus-i-kit. Mus-i-cat. Mus-i-cal. Musical!"

It was the tenth word I'd finally gotten right in the past half hour. Now I was tired. Who would have thought that simple speech could be so exhausting?

Regaining motion was another effort entirely: flexing my fingers, toes, and feet. Making them strong and able to do my bidding.

"Can't be my sinature! Like a first-graver's."

"You're doing fine, Sharon. Let's work on signing your name a few more times." Jill Hughes, one of my physical therapists, was annoyingly upbeat.

"You ever a sheerleader?" I asked.

"A what?"

I paused and shaped my mouth to make the word come out right. "Cheerleader."

"What's that got to do with—"

I shook my head and picked up the pen that I'd thrown down on the table. "Try sinning again."

Jill's eyes met mine, and we both started to laugh.

And so it went, until the day when my words made sense, but the voice and inflections didn't sound like my own.

"Better today," I told Phoebe after she'd returned from a long weekend. It was a flat statement that didn't reflect the excitement and hope I felt inside.

"Very good!"

"Been practick...practicing those speech exercises you gave me." I demonstrated shaping words with exaggerated mouth and tongue motions. "Nighttime, maybe three hours." I felt as if a stranger were talking through me.

"You've made a lot of progress. Are you ready to work even harder?"

"Yes."

"Then let's get started. Why don't you read me the lead article in the *Chronicle*?"

I picked up that morning's newspaper with fingers that no longer fumbled. " 'Yesterday Presh...President Barack Obama...unequiv-ocally stated...' "

The news, at least for today, was good.

I spent hours toning my long unused muscles until I had control over them.

"Let's turn over on our side," Mark Ito, physical therapist, said.

From my position on my back on the padded table I stared up at the ceiling and sighed. My breakfast had been oatmeal, which I'd despised since my childhood when my mother insisted I start every day with it. I'd accidentally looked at the bathroom mirror and seen my nearly bald head. A phone call from Elwood Farmer, my birth father who lived on the Flathead Rez in Montana, had annoyed me: he was doing what I thought of as his mystical Indian shtick today, quoting Shoshone proverbs that didn't have much to do with my current problematical situation. I asked him not to try so hard to be a father at this late date—we'd only discovered each other a few years ago—and instead of taking offense, he'd waxed more eloquent and philosophical. I'd hung up on him. Later I would have to mend fences.

Mark Ito repeated, "Let's turn over on our side now."

"Whose side? Yours or mine?"

"Testy today, aren't we?"

"I am. I don't know about you."

"On our side, please." He motioned but refrained from helping me.

I thumped onto my side, feeling as a walrus must. God, was I gaining weight? That would add the final insult to injury!

"That's good," Mark said. "Now let's raise our right knee.... Very good. We're doing fine."

"Maybe *you* are. This hurts."

"Testiness is a sign of healing."

And then there was the walking: a halting step; an assisted journey down the hospital's corridor, clinging to a railing.

"What's this thing around me, Mark? A harness?"

"So you won't fall. I've got you. Grasp the bar on the wall and stabilize yourself. Then take a step with your right foot."

"Not *our* right foot?"

"I got your message weeks ago: no PT speak. Step, please."

I stepped, teetered some. Mark pulled on the harness to steady me.

"I feel like a toy poodle being taken for a walk."

"One more step."

I took two. "Betcha I can outrun a toy poodle."

"Try two more."

I took three.

Finally I walked slowly on my own down that same corridor.

"Hey, look at you, Shar!" Mark began applauding. "Hey, every-body," he called to others in the hallway, "look at McCone!"

Two orderlies, a nurse, and a patient in a wheelchair joined in Mark's applause.

"Thank you." I made a slight bow. "I'm stepping out."

As I made my way toward the lobby and the bench outside the front door, where my nurse had frequently wheeled me in my chair, my eyes filled with tears of gratitude for all the Institute staff had done for me.

Eventually there was a day in December when I heard myself talk-ing as I always had, and the two halves of my verbal ability became one.

"I've been thinking, Ripinsky," I said to Hy. We were relaxing in front of the kiva-style fireplace in the sitting room at our Church Street house. Home for good, at last.

"About what?"

"I ought to start putting in appearances at the office, if only for the staff meetings." McCone Investigations had been in the hands of my capable employees for nearly five months now, but I missed the day-to-day involvement. "Things're okay, but they need me."

"I thought you weren't going back till after the first of the year. You don't want to overdo it."

"Dammit, Ripinsky, I'm sick of being an invalid! I want my fuckin' life back!"

He grinned widely, white teeth flashing beneath his bushy dark blond mustache. "I'd say you're well on your way, colorful vocabulary and all."

When the Brandt Institute released me from their therapy program they referred me to a rehab center in the Inner Sunset district. It was quite a distance from my house and the pier, but I went six or seven days a week, and gradually I became more and more the person I used to be.

It would be over six months before the state of California would allow me to operate a motor vehicle: people who have had seizures and brain damage must serve a probationary period after recovery. It would be nearly a year or more before an FAA-certified doctor would sign off on my medical status and even longer until I proved my abilities to their examiners and my pilot's license was restored.

But all of that would happen. With hard work and determination I'd come all the way back.

Others, I knew, were not so fortunate.

FRIDAY, FEBRUARY 6

SHARON McCONE

W hen Piper Quinn didn't make it to our exercise session for the fifth straight day, I got worried.

I'd met Piper at the Brandt Neurological Institute, where she'd also been a patient, and when she'd been released from their therapy program she'd joined me for daily sessions at Alta Vista Rehab, on Judah Street near the UC medical campus. The center was like a gym, with trainers who were specialists in various disorders and injuries; it even had a pool and a juice bar. A staff doctor designed an individual program for each patient—only they called us clients—and Piper and I reconnected at the weight machines.

Piper's condition made mine seem like a common cold: two years ago she'd been hit by a speeding car while crossing with the light at the intersection of Geary Boulevard and Seventeenth Avenue. The force of the impact threw her some twenty yards through the window of a storefront. The driver of the car was probably drunk; he hadn't even slowed down, much less stopped to help.

The combination of broken arms and legs and ribs, extreme blood loss, a collapsed lung, and some brain damage resulting in a coma should have killed her. As should the stroke that paralyzed the right side of her body after she regained consciousness. But Piper was young—twenty-seven—and strong and loved life. She clung to it ferociously. After six operations and two months in acute care at San Francisco General, she was admitted to the Brandt Institute, where she gradually reclaimed what she could.

Piper would always walk with a cane and a limp and sometimes slur or scramble her words. She would always seem a bit "off" to so-called normal people. But she was pretty and vibrant and determined to succeed at whatever she attempted to do. A survivor like no other.

That was why her repeated absences from our exercise sessions gave me cause for concern.

I stood on the sidewalk watching the N-Judah streetcar pull away from the nearby stop. A common sight, the rear end of public transit vehicles; they were never there when I needed them. For most of the time I'd lived in the city I'd zipped around in my vintage red MG, a great car to weave through traffic and wedge into tiny parking spaces. Now, because I couldn't drive till the doctors and the DMV gave me the go-ahead next July, my choice was to rely on the Muni rather than my husband and my friends and associates. I hated asking favors and wanted to guard my independence, so I spent a lot of money on the Muni—there had been a recent fare hike—and an inordinate amount of time at bus and streetcar stops.

Now I checked my watch. Four-thirteen. Hy would be in his South-of-Market office at RI, the corporate security firm he owned; in the time it would take him to get here through Friday rush hour traffic, it would be five-thirty or six. Our caseload at the agency was light these days—although not so light as to cause alarm—and my employees had been leaving early; I didn't want to keep them from their weekend.

I fingered the pendant I wore over my sweater, a single large multicolored opal—turquoise, green, blue, and fiery red. I'd worn it every day this week to show Piper how much I appreciated her gift. She'd been wearing it last Friday when we had coffee at the little café on the corner, and when I admired it she said, "If you like it, I want you to have it."

I protested, but she took the pendant off and fastened it around my neck, saying, "It was a present from an old love. He bought it intending to win me back. Not possible now." I loved the pendant and had shown it off to everybody at the office, but Piper had yet to see me wear it.

Now I reached into my backpack for my PDA and accessed Piper's address, three blocks away on Tenth Avenue. That was all the contact information I had for her; for two people who had grown so emotionally close, we'd never exchanged phone numbers or e-mail addresses. And now that I thought of it, that had been her doing. She shied away from any connection outside the rehab center, except for the occasional cup of coffee at the café, where we talked of our progress or neutral subjects.

I knew very little about her life. Our friendship revolved around our disabilities.

I did know that she was from the Midwest but had left there eight years before to attend a now-defunct computer graphics school in Santa Cruz. Her degree led to a job offer to manage a Web site for a clothing firm here in the city, and later she'd moved along to another, similar position in what she called the rag trade. After three years, she had the connections and know-how to establish her own firm, which she ran out of her apartment. She'd been returning to her car from a meeting with a client when she crossed Geary and was struck by the hit-and-run driver.

What I didn't know about Piper would fill volumes. What had her childhood been like? Were her parents still living? Did she have siblings? Friends? A boyfriend other than the "old love"? Had she ever been married? Had a child? She'd had few visitors at Brandt and those that came had not stayed long. One, she'd told me, was her attorney. Another, a neighbor bringing her some things she needed from her apartment. It was as if the accident had severed her personal time line, leaving Before on one side and After on the other.

She'd gotten back to work once she left the Institute,

reconnecting with a few old clients and getting referrals from them to others, and she spoke enthusiastically of her projects. I sensed she was more concerned about doing something useful than the money it brought in; she'd received a large insurance payment from her accident policy with State Farm, which had taken care of her medical bills plus allowed her to maintain her apartment during her recovery. Maybe she had money of her own—savings or a trust fund. She never acted as if she were on the brink of financial disaster, as so many of the people who came to Alta Vista Rehab did.

I hesitated a moment more on the sidewalk, craning my neck to see if a streetcar was in sight, then decided on impulse to pay Piper a visit. I was worried about her, and as an excuse for just dropping in I could tell her I needed a place to wait till Hy was available.

I set out for Tenth Avenue.

The buildings on Piper's block were a mixture of brick Edwardians, stucco cottages, and three-story modern apartments of a similar bay-windowed style. Cars clogged the curbs, motorcycles wedged between them, and bicycles were chained to railings and lampposts. Too few garages, too many people. It was a bland area, except for the occasional garish purple or pink house, and now rendered gray by the fog and fading light.

Piper's address was one of the modern structures. Three mailboxes, three buzzers and intercoms. Her unit, naturally, was on the ground floor, and a wheelchair ramp spanned part of the front steps. She used the chair on days when walking was too much for her.

I rang the bell but received no answering buzz. Then I saw that the lobby door was partly open; somebody had wedged a newspaper between it and the jamb. I went in and spotted Piper's door at the back of the lobby, next to the stairs; it was also partway open. As I entered a long narrow hallway with three closed doors leading off it, I called out to Piper.

Silence.

I went along the hallway, glancing at the prints on the walls: Chinese scenes of mountains towering over villages or lone houses, executed in intricate detail. Reducing everyday life to something small and manageable. I wondered if Piper had selected them before or after her accident. Probably I was reading too much into her choice of artwork, but since being shot I'd found that small and manageable worked for me.

The hallway widened out into a living room with a blue plush sofa and two matching chairs arranged before a gas-log fireplace. Lighter blue curtains were closed against the fog and a table lamp burned low. Piper lay on her side on the sofa, wearing a long white robe; the flicker of the flames accentuated her high cheekbones and picked out red-gold streaks in her long blonde hair. One arm trailed off the sofa, its fingers grazing the gray carpet. She didn't move or acknowledge my presence.

I went over and touched her shoulder lightly, so as not to alarm her. She stirred, muttered, and went still again.

Oh God, I thought, *relapse. Another seizure or stroke. How many times have I been afraid that would happen to me?*

"Piper." I spoke softly.

No response.

"Piper!" I shook her shoulder.

Her eyes opened slowly, dull and unfocused.

"It's me—Sharon."

"Uhhh...Sharon." She tried to raise her extended arm, but it fell back.

"Piper, what happened? Are you all right?"

"Huh? Oh..." She closed her eyes, swallowed heavily.

"I'll call the EMTs—"

"No. You...help me. Problem I can't control."

"What problem?"

"Um..."

"Piper, tell me!"

"Your job, you know…"

"What about my job?"

She sank back into a stupor.

I shook her again. No response. I lifted one of her eyelids; her pupils were dilated to the max.

Drugged.

I looked around for a pill bottle, a syringe. Nothing.

I was about to call 911 on my cell when there was a noise at the end of the hall, the sound of the outer door closing. A tall, middle-aged woman with short gray hair and round dark-framed glasses appeared, grocery bag in hand. The glasses and her slightly hooked nose reminded me of an owl. She was dressed unseasonably in a T-shirt and shorts; her legs and arms were sinewy and tanned. Probably a runner.

She stopped and looked from me to Piper and back to me. "Well," she said, "what's this?"

I introduced myself as Piper's friend from Alta Vista Rehab. "I was about to call 911. Piper's out of it; it looks as if she's taken an overdose of drugs."

The woman glanced at Piper. Behind her glasses her eyes moved shrewdly, assessing the situation.

After a few beats she said in a faint drawl, "I'm sure she'll be fine. She's a diabetic, you know, and isn't good about taking her meds. I'll give her an insulin shot and she'll perk right up."

I found that explanation hard to believe. Piper had never mentioned diabetes, and even if she had the disease, I couldn't imagine her ever neglecting her medications.

The woman set down the grocery bag on the nearby dining table and went to Piper. "Upsy-daisy, honey. Let's get you into the bedroom." She lifted her with ease and pushed through one of the closed doors, shutting it behind her.

I went over there and listened, but couldn't make out anything. Shortly the woman reappeared. "She'll be okay now."

I asked, "And you are?"

Hesitation. Then, "Melinda Knowles, a friend from back home. Piper's aunt, actually."

"How long have you been visiting?"

"Oh, just a few days. I came west to help out."

Why hadn't she come before this, when Piper really could have used help? Why now, when Piper had regained her independence?

"Came out from where?" I asked.

She moved closer to me and began herding me toward the hallway, in a series of little, nipping invasions of my space designed for that purpose.

"You're from where?" I repeated.

Knowles kept herding me. I held my ground till we were close enough that I could feel her breath on my face. I caught the scent of mint overlying alcohol. An early happy hour?

Finally she said, "I'm from a little town near Oklahoma City. You wouldn't know of it."

Now I placed her accent—not Southern or Texan, but distinctive in its own way. "The town where Piper is from?"

My guess was right. Knowles nodded. "If she'd stayed home, this awful thing never would have happened to her."

"I'd like to look in on her for a moment."

"No, she needs her rest. And I need to get dinner on the table. She has to have her nourishment on a regular basis."

But Piper was perfectly capable of providing her own meals. Just last week she'd told me about a complicated soufflé that she'd cooked.

I hesitated, reluctant to leave her alone with this woman who so obviously wanted me gone.

Knowles's face softened. "I know you're worried about Piper. I am too. She was doing so well until this week."

"What happened?"

"I'm not sure. She won't talk about it."

"A shock of some kind?"

"Maybe. I'll ask her to call you when she's better."

"Thank you." Then I realized Piper didn't have my number, and I gave Knowles one of my business cards. She set it on an end table, barely glancing at it.

"I'm sure Piper will be glad you stopped by," Knowles said, ushering me to the door, her movements no longer so aggressive.

Still I hesitated. This woman reminded me of a watchdog, and not the benign kind.

"Good-bye for now," she said.

I stepped into the hall and the door closed behind me, the dead bolt clicking into place.

HY RIPINSKY

He loved Shar, but she could be a pain in the ass sometimes. Like tonight: dragging into the house at nearly seven after taking two streetcars from the rehab center. She'd told him she'd had an upsetting experience and needed time by herself to process it, but she didn't want to discuss it just yet.

Bullshitting him, probably. The Muni was not a place to do any serious thinking. Just an excuse for her damned stubborn insistence on being independent.

He'd told her as much, and she'd disappeared downstairs to their bedroom suite to take a shower. Moving more slowly than normal; the long rides—probably standing up—had tired her.

He grabbed an IPA from the fridge and sat down in front of the fire to wait for her.

The last few months had been hard on him—a conflicted time. What he'd most valued in his wife when they first met, her self-sufficiency and bravery, were taxing his patience. Scaring him a little too. She'd come a long way since last July, when she'd been delivered by a gifted neurosurgeon from a life in a locked-in state, and most times she seemed like her old self.

Well, except for her hair: it had grown back thick and black as before, but it was short and spiky and there was a weird white streak that she complained made her look like a skunk. She'd had a small gray streak in the same place since her teens, which she dyed, but she refused to color this one till her hair grew out. People joked about her new look, and she laughed, but he knew her appearance bothered her.

It certainly didn't bother him. It was the pushing of her limits that did. If as a result something happened to her...

He'd had experience with disability before: his first wife, Julie Spaulding, had died of multiple sclerosis. But Julie had been ill before he married her and had learned to live with the disease. She knew her limits and didn't exceed them and, as a consequence, Hy had made his own accommodations.

Julie, he thought now. Something she'd said about being disabled flickered in Hy's memory, then vanished. He tried to recapture it but couldn't. Julie had been gone many years, and the small details of their life together had faded. Some of the bigger ones, too, he hated to admit.

He heard Shar coming up the spiral staircase from the bedroom and went to the kitchen to fetch her a glass of chardonnay. By the time he was back in the sitting room, she had sunk onto the sofa and pulled a soft woolen blanket around her. Her hair was wet from the shower, her cheeks rosy. He handed her the glass and said, "Better now?"

"Yes." She sipped, smiled at him. Their spats were infrequent and short; neither could stay angry with the other.

But, dammit, she had to understand how he'd felt: alone, unsure where she was and if she was all right. She hadn't even given him the courtesy of a phone call.

"My cell discharged," she said.

Reading his mind; they'd always had that connection, even at a long physical distance.

"And there aren't many phone booths around anymore."

He put his hand on her knee, enjoying the solid feel of flesh and bone. "I know."

"The damn thing's unreliable," she added, looking down into her wineglass. "My cell, I mean."

"Buy a better one. Or keep it on the charger when you're home."

"I know I should. But I..." Her voice trailed off into silence. "It's hard," she added, "getting around to things like that."

"I understand."

"And sometimes it's a relief to be unavailable. My mother, my brother, John. Charlene and Patsy too. The only ones who don't want to caution me to take it easy a dozen times a day are my birth family. At least they trust me."

"Your mother and brother and sisters care."

"That's not the point! They view me as infirm, somebody who's not capable of getting on with her life. Ma left seven messages at the agency today. Seven! John's down to five, Patsy and Charlene two apiece. But I bet there're more on the voice mail here."

"Well, not exactly. When I got home there were a few from your mother and John. I called them back with my daily report."

"*You've* gotten sucked into reassuring them too?" Her face was scrunched up, her eyes flashing.

Mildly he said, "They're family, McCone. The only family I've got except for you."

Her eyes softened and her mouth pulled down.

God, he thought, *now I've gone and made her feel sorry for me!*

But he knew that wasn't quite right: his parents and stepfather had been dead many years; Shar knew he'd gotten on fine, never been really close to them.

He put his arm around her. "Hey, McCone," he said, "what's made you so blue?"

She took a sip of wine and patted the sofa for their sole remaining cat, Allie—her brother, Ralph, had died peacefully of old age in November—to jump into her lap. Then she told him about her visit to Piper Quinn.

"I just can't understand what's happened to her. I'm sure she doesn't have diabetes and that she'd never willingly take recreational drugs, but something's very wrong, something so bad the

Knowles woman came out here from Oklahoma. She seems to be very protective of Piper. In fact, it's as if she's taking over her life."

He was silent, considering the situation.

"So what do you think I should do about Piper?"

"Nothing."

"Nothing? Ripinsky, the woman's in trouble! She asked for my help with a problem."

"Maybe it was the drugs—whatever they were—talking."

"...Maybe, but...She mentioned my job. What if she needs the agency's help?"

"It doesn't sound as if an investigation is required. You admit you don't know much about her."

"True."

"She's probably just going through a bad patch. Rehab, as you know, isn't always a straight upward trajectory."

"I know."

"So let it go. The aunt seems to have everything in hand."

McCone's brow furrowed. Hy felt faintly guilty about his advice: his wife's instincts were excellent, but he was deliberately steering her away from getting involved.

He thought of all she'd been through, how far she'd come, how important it was for her to maintain the status quo. He touched her hair, brushing the white streak.

"Look, haven't you had enough stress recently? How about we fly up to Touchstone tomorrow? Look at the sunset, eat some fresh crab, relax?"

Her expression softened, was replaced with one of longing. They hadn't visited their seaside retreat in Mendocino County since before the shooting.

After a moment she said, "On Monday, if Piper's not at the rehab center, I'll visit her again. Get to the bottom of what's going on."

He pulled her close. "Monday's soon enough."

SATURDAY, FEBRUARY 7

MICK SAVAGE

He and Derek Ford were going over their software licensing contracts with Omnivore when his cell rang. He ignored it, let the call go into voice mail.

They were sitting side by side on the futon couch in Derek's tiny SoMa loft, the contracts for the real-time search engine—SavageFor.com—that they'd developed spread out on a low table before them.

Real-time searches were the hottest trend in the Internet industry; a number of them were already up and running, but Mick and Derek's tapped into a much wider and more reliable range of resources to bring people up to the minute on what was happening in the world. From *TIME* magazine to Twitter, from CNN to personal blogs, information was gathered, posted, and updated by the second. Omnivore would oversee and maintain the site, leaving Mick and Derek to follow their other pursuits.

Derek's loft was one of the kind that you bought with only the electrical and plumbing in place, then finished yourself. He'd done a good job: bamboo floors and a small but convenient kitchen nook. A little spare for Mick's taste—no pictures on the white walls, nothing but a computer workstation that took up half the space, the futon, and the table. But Derek was a minimalist and spent most of his downtime at the clubs or various women's places.

Mick wished he could get as much action as Derek apparently did.

"This clause needs rewording," Derek said, running a long slender finger over a highlighted passage.

Mick read it, shrugged. "Let the lawyers deal with it."

Derek frowned. He was a tall, slender Eurasian—Vietnamese, American, French, and Chinese—and always perfectly groomed and dressed. A tat of linked scorpions circled his neck. For years, Mick knew, Derek had lived beyond his means and had the credit card balances to prove it.

Well, once the contracts were signed he would easily be able to afford the silk shirts and leather jackets and pricey shoes he favored.

Derek said, "Hey, man, it's our future we're talking about. We ought to work on the wording."

"I don't know shit about this kind of stuff."

"Neither do I."

"So leave it to the lawyers."

"Right. Leave it to the lawyers. You want a beer?"

"Sure."

Mick's phone rang again. He ignored it. The ringing stopped, then immediately started. He checked it, noted Shar and Hy's number at Touchstone. A prickle of anxiety touched his spine. What if something had happened to his aunt? She was okay, the doctors claimed, but wasn't anything possible? Even a relapse?

He picked up. No, she told him, sounding a touch testy, she was feeling fine. "The reason I'm calling is I need you to run a deep background check on a couple of people," she added.

"You sound as if you're in a cave."

"I'm in the pantry with the door closed."

"Why're you calling from the pantry? Gorging on canned goods?"

"Hy and I are supposed to be on a getaway, but... This is really important, Mick."

"Okay. Which case file?"

"None of them. It's personal."

What kind of situation had she gotten herself into now? She'd been coming into the office on a semi-regular basis since December, but as far as he knew she wasn't handling any cases except for being a chief witness in a big federal appeals trial that would go to court next month. But with Shar many so-called personal cases turned into official investigations—usually major ones with major consequences. Was she up for something like that?

"You gonna tell me why you don't want Hy to know you're calling?"

"No. Will you do it or not?"

Yep, stubborn as ever and off on some wild-hair investigation over Hy's objections.

"You're handling the testimony in the Andersen Associates appeal," he said. "You've got a lot on your plate."

When she replied her voice was tart and steely. "I know my capabilities, Mick."

Maybe, maybe not.

Shar had always stretched herself to the limit, but was that wise now? But if Mick didn't run the check, she'd do it herself, and then she and Hy would get into a big fight on their supposed romantic weekend.

"All right," he said. "Give me the information."

SUNDAY, FEBRUARY 8

SHARON McCONE

The getaway weekend wasn't a success.

First of all, Allie the cat acted mournful as we packed some provisions on Saturday morning. She and Ralph had always recognized the signs that we were going away, but before they'd had each other, and now she'd be all alone. I called next door to Michelle Curley, my house- and cat-sitter, and asked if Allie could stay with her while we were gone. As I carried the cat over there she felt bony and frail, and I sensed impending loss.

The flight up from Oakland's North Field to our airstrip at Touchstone only reinforced the feeling. I watched Hy at the controls of our Cessna 170B: his motions so precise, so easy. When I followed them through from the right seat—my hands light on the yoke, my feet light on the rudders—I became confused, clumsy.

Was it possible I'd never pilot well again? Or never pilot at all? That was unthinkable.

Our house at Touchstone was musty and damp. Mold lurked in the shower stall and the bedroom hot tub looked scummy. The ice maker had seized up. Outside the sea was gray and curiously placid; a thick bank of fog menaced on the horizon. The crab season hadn't been good, and the ones we'd picked up at our favorite seafood market in Mendocino were small and tasteless.

Saturday morning I didn't feel up to climbing down the long stairway that scaled the cliff from our property to Bootleggers'

Cove below. To tell the truth, I wasn't sure I'd ever descend it again.

That afternoon, Hy spied me coming out of the pantry with the cordless phone after I talked with Mick. He didn't comment—a sure indication that he was onto me but didn't want to initiate any conflict.

Jesus, I was sick of being treated as if I were special!

Special—as in "special needs."

No, handicapped. Less than my former self.

When I woke Sunday morning, I was alone in bed. I put on my robe, moved through the house. No Hy. Then I spotted him on the platform above the stairway, staring out to sea, a coffee cup balanced on the railing before him.

I wondered what he was thinking of. The sea, its constancy? How different it was from our life together, with all its changes?

In an instant what we'd both taken for granted had been destroyed. What was possible had become the impossible. The landscape of our existence was forever altered. He and I didn't recognize this new, strange world—a world of "no's" and "can'ts" and "shouldn'ts." Didn't *want* to recognize it.

And as I watched my husband I realized he and I hadn't made love all weekend—or all the week before. Good and frequent sex was one of the cornerstones of our relationship; now, apparently, that was altered too.

When I'd first been released from the Brandt Institute, we—with some difficulty—had resumed and enjoyed sexual relations, but our interest hadn't lasted long. Now we were both indifferent.

What had happened to us? And where were we going?

On the trip back to the Bay Area I slept—ignoring the controls, Hy's piloting, and the 360 degrees of striking vistas. When I woke upon our touchdown at Oakland, I felt as if I'd lost some essential part of myself in the skies above.

MONDAY, FEBRUARY 9

TED SMALLEY

The ficus tree in Shar's office at the end of the pier was dying—which was strange for a fake plant. Leaves cascaded over the armchair by the big arching window overlooking the bay and littered the beige carpet. He picked one up: it felt brittle. Well, silk didn't last forever; probably it had dried up from too much sun. He'd check into how much it would cost to replace it.

He knew a fair amount about silk now, since he'd decided to make it his next fashion statement. A crash course on the Internet and a discussion with Derek had informed him it would be an expensive proposition, but it was his last resort. Over the years since he graduated from Penn and moved to San Francisco he'd gone through a retro hippie period (bare feet and shaggy hair); an Edwardian phase (velvet frock coats and jeans); a professorial look (tweed jackets with elbow patches and cords); a grunge stage (torn jeans and ripped tees), a junior executive suit-and-tie shtick (*that* had lasted only six weeks), a Hawaiian shirt craze (he'd loved it, his longest); and two years of cowboying (Western wear, complete with boots and hat and now growing stale). He'd also made detours into leather, Goth, all-cotton casual, and lurid polyester, but none had lasted long.

To tell the truth, coming up with new looks was wearying. He continued only because his friends and his life partner, Neal Osborn, expected it of him. Maybe if he liked the silk statement he'd stick with it, or go back to Hawaiian. One thing for sure, he wasn't reprising grunge.

He was still standing by the window musing over silk when Shar came in. She looked terrible.

Not terrible meaning sick, but tired and on edge and slightly unkempt. Of course, until her hair grew out fully, she was bound not to look her best.

She set her briefcase down on her desk with a thud. Glanced at him and said, "What're you doing here?"

No usual pleasant greeting. Wound tight, and it would only get worse as the day progressed. Common sense told him to make a speedy exit.

Common sense did not prevail.

"The ficus," he said, "it's dying."

She snorted, lowered herself—painfully, it seemed to him—into her desk chair. "How can a fake plant die?"

"The light's pretty intense. It's dried up."

"So throw the thing out."

"I can check on replacement costs—"

"Ted, that plant was expensive five years ago. This agency is not exactly minting money right now."

"Well, what about a real one?"

She was riffling through the briefcase, not finding whatever she was after. "Who the hell is going to feed and water a plant?"

"Kendra would be glad to. She's growing a beautiful orchid on her desk." Kendra Williams, his assistant—the Paragon of the Paper Clips, he called her, but her skills ranged far and wide.

"Kendra has better things to do." She left off rummaging in the briefcase, bowed her head, and folded her hands, began breathing deeply. After a moment she said, "Sorry. Rough morning. I didn't mean to take it out on you."

"What's wrong?"

"My cat died in her sleep last night. Allie."

Allie—the calico that, along with her butterscotch littermate

Ralph, Shar had adopted as kittens years ago. They'd been an unwise gift from a well-meaning friend of Ted's buddy Harry, shortly before Harry died of AIDS. Ted felt a twinge, remembering the little rambunctious furballs and the affectionate adult cats they'd become. He put his hand on her shoulder. "I'm so sorry."

"Thanks."

"We'll talk later. You need some time to get yourself sorted out."

"Yeah, I do."

Ted moved toward the door, but Shar's voice stopped him. "Ted, get a real plant, would you? And thank Kendra in advance for tending to it."

ADAH JOSLYN

Okay, she thought, initialing an invoice, that's the lot of them. Now she could get around to that stack of reports and then review the week's assignments with Patrick. Desk work she was used to: as a homicide investigator with the SFPD she'd spent a lot of time in the field—grueling time that had taxed her emotions and her very soul. But always there'd been the reports and other paperwork. This job, it seemed like her former one cut in half.

And she didn't have to worry about being summoned on an almost daily basis to yet another ugly crime scene.

As she pulled the pile of reports toward her she sensed a presence. She looked over her shoulder and saw Ted in the doorway. His fine features were sad, his salt-and-pepper hair and goatee unkempt, as if he'd been clawing at them.

"You all right?" she asked.

"I am. Shar's not."

Alarm shot through her. "Oh, God, not a relapse—"

"No. Her cat died."

To someone else it might've been an anticlimactic statement. But Adah was a lifelong cat lover, had cried on and off for days when her fat old Charley bought it. And she would be similarly devastated if she were to lose either That One and The Other One—abbreviated to One and Other—even though she and Craig had adopted the young tortoiseshells only a short time ago.

"How's Shar taking it?"

"Not well, but she'll be okay."

"Maybe we should suggest she take the day off."

"That's the last thing she needs, being made to feel expendable."

"I don't understand."

Ted moved out of the doorway, went around the desk, and sat across from her.

"Shar needs to feel she's in charge here. She gave up the daily stuff to you—and she wanted to, even before she was shot—but she's still the boss."

"I know that."

"Well, a lot of the time you don't treat her that way. You act as if she's some...cripple we keep on staff because she needs a job."

"What!"

"That's what I see, Adah."

"Look, she's handling the appeal on the Andersen case. There's a lot riding on that, and she knows it."

"Because you've impressed it on her several times in staff meetings: 'Are you sure you're up to it, Shar? Do you need help?'"

Adah replayed the tape in her mind. Ted was right—she'd been just short of patronizing.

"Cut her some slack, Adah. Like she cut you some when you had that meltdown years ago."

God, she didn't want to be reminded of that time! Assigned as a liaison by the PD to a special FBI task force where she wasn't welcomed. Alternately bullied and dismissed by the all-male field agents. Finally she'd cracked under the pressure, lashed out, crashed and burned. Shar—and Craig, then the only member of the task force who'd been remotely decent to her—had been her rocks. Afterward she'd pulled herself together and vowed never to let her emotions get the better of her again.

But her experience had been different from Shar's, whose occasional lapses into confusion and forgetfulness stemmed from much more serious roots. And it hadn't helped that since Shar's return to work, none of the clients who had contracted with the agency presented problems serious or complex enough to intrigue her. The whole point of turning over the administrative work to Adah was so Shar could be free to work on the bigger cases, but none had come their way. No wonder the lapses: she must be bored out of her mind.

"Okay," Adah said to Ted. "I hear you."

"I knew you would."

"Oh, did you? Why?"

"Because everybody around this place listens to the Grand Poobah."

CRAIG MORLAND

He sent a silly text message to Adah, one of the kind that people in love do: "U R so great. C U 2nite."

Then he went along the catwalk to the office of Thelia Chen, the agency's financial expert, shared with Patrick Neilan, the operative who coordinated the firm's investigations. Patrick—red haired, freckled, with badly rumpled clothing—was writing on one of his whiteboard flow charts and stealing glances at Thelia—a petite woman, with straight black hair that flowed nearly to her waist and exquisite facial features. She was totally focused on her computer screen.

Patrick, Craig knew, secretly lusted after Thelia, but she came encumbered with a doctor husband and daughters aged seven and ten. And Patrick came encumbered too—a divorced father with sole custody of boys aged eight and nine. Caring for them, plus the heavy demands of his job, had pretty much put a chill on the romance department: every time he met someone unattached whom he was attracted to, she took one look at the Neilan ménage and bolted.

"Thelia," Craig said, taking a seat in the spare chair, "I've just been going over the Andersen Associates appeals file. It looks solid to me. Do you think there's anything we've overlooked?"

Andersen Associates was a defense contractor that had been convicted of bilking the government out of nearly ninety million dollars on contracts for rebuilding the infrastructure of Kabul, Afghanistan. Thelia's initial investigation had revealed the accusation to be suspect; Shar's deeper inquiry had indicated that the Internet blogger who first published the exposé and a chief witness for the prosecution had colluded in altering evidence for personal gain. The appeal was scheduled for next month.

"If we'd missed anything, their lawyers would've caught it. How come you're concerned with Andersen?" Chen asked, not taking her eyes off the monitor.

"Adah asked me to prep on it, in case Shar can't handle the testimony."

"Why wouldn't she?"

"Well, she conducted her investigation over a year ago. Before she was shot."

"And?"

"Adah thought she might not make the most reliable witness."

"Why?"

"Sometimes she's not as quick as she used to be. And she forgets details."

Thelia swiveled to face him, removing her round glasses and looking severe. "There's nothing wrong with her memory or grasp of the facts, Craig. And the reason she's not always quick is that she tires easily."

"Right. Adah's afraid she could get rattled on the stand, lose it—"

"I doubt that's going to happen. She'll be fully prepared and rested."

"I don't know. Adah was thinking maybe I should take over her testimony. Or you should."

"Shar's the one who did most of the work. I only provided preliminary data. And you weren't involved at all. The judge wants to hear from the primary investigator."

He couldn't think of an immediate response.

"Anyway," Chen went on, "it's not Adah's call. An executive

administrator doesn't make decisions like that. If anyone other than Shar should, it's Patrick."

He looked up from his chart and raised his hands. "I just keep track of where things're going. I don't assign which people should do them."

"If you ask me," Chen added, "you and Adah are trying to usurp Shar's responsibilities. I've heard a lot of negative talk around here about how she's not the woman she used to be. And in some ways she isn't: she has emotional as well as physical problems to overcome. But she's making great progress and is perfectly capable of handling this testimony."

"Why're you so sure of that? You haven't been with the agency very long. You don't know her the way Adah and I do."

Chen's eyes narrowed; they looked much like Adah's when she was taking Craig to task for some transgression.

She said, "My husband, Keith? You know he's a neurologist at UC Med Center."

Craig nodded.

"After Shar was released from Brandt she went to him for a second opinion on how she was doing. He confirmed everything Dr. Saxnay at the Institute said. She only has to believe in herself, and she's going to be fine."

"But *does* she believe?"

"It's up to those of us who care for her to make sure she does." Chen turned back to her computer.

Why did he feel like a kid who'd been chastised for something he hadn't done? Craig looked at Patrick, who shrugged.

He got up and left the office. Despite Chen's opinion, he planned to continue to familiarize himself with the Andersen Associates file.

SHARON McCONE

Mick's e-mailed report on Piper Quinn and Melinda Knowles was in my in-box at around ten-thirty. The note appended to it said he was sorry for not transmitting it sooner, but he'd had a late breakfast meeting with a client and then wanted to verify a few facts after coming into the office. The delay was irritating, but I didn't express that in my return note. No use taking out my grief for Allie on others. Besides, Mick *had* worked on the weekend.

What he'd found out was intriguing.

The basic facts about Piper were unsurprising. Born in Denver to Catharine and James Quinn, both deceased. Mainly raised in Homewood, a suburb of Oklahoma City. An only child. Graduated Homewood High School and the Academy of Computer Graphics in Santa Cruz. Sole proprietor, Quinn Graphics, San Francisco.

Nothing there I wouldn't have guessed, and the deceased parents and lack of siblings told me why no relative had come to see her at Brandt. I turned to the next page of the detailed report. Piper had been married six years ago to Ryan Middleton, a marine stationed at Camp Pendleton in Southern California; the couple had made minor news because their wedding had been sparked by winning a cruise to Mexico in a supermarket-opening raffle. They lived together intermittently for two years, then Middleton was deployed to Iraq. A year ago, Piper had petitioned for a divorce, citing irreconcilable differences.

Why, I wondered? Well, the marriage had been long-distance from the first and then he'd undertaken a second tour of duty in the Middle East. Those conditions more than constituted a breakdown in the relationship.

It was a moot point, because Middleton never returned the divorce papers. And seven months ago, he and two other marine officers were killed by a suicide bomber outside an office building in Mosul, the country's third-largest city and a turbulent stronghold for Sunni insurgents. His flag-draped coffin joined the steady stream of those coming back to be buried in military cemeteries across the nation—in his case, Holy Cross in Colma, south of San Francisco. His wife was still in the Brandt Institute at the time and unable to attend the interment. The final notation in his service jacket was that his personal effects had been shipped to Piper.

No wonder she didn't like to talk about the past.

I skimmed through the rest of the report, mostly backgrounding on Piper's accident, nothing I didn't already know, then turned to the one on Melinda Knowles.

She didn't exist. At least in relation to Piper.

Lots of Melinda Knowleses across the country, but none in Homewood, Oklahoma. None of her approximate age in the entire state. I shut my eyes and reviewed my conversation with her:

"I'm from a little town near Oklahoma City. You wouldn't know of it."

"The town where Piper is from?"

"...If she'd stayed home, this awful thing never would have happened to her."

Yes, Knowles had represented herself as being from Piper's hometown. I flipped back to the report on Piper: no mention of an aunt living in Homewood or anyplace else. I sent a quick e-mail to Mick, thanking him and asking him to dig deeper on Knowles and get preliminary background on Ryan Middleton, then left the office.

I wouldn't wait to see if Piper made it to rehab today. I'd check on her now.

As I went past Ted's office, he called out, "Three messages from your mother, one from John."

I kept going.

Fortunately I could catch the N-Judah streetcar at a close-by stop on the Embarcadero. As I sat, watching the bayside morph to downtown and then the Castro district and into the suburban-feeling inner Sunset, I reflected that there must be a better way to get around town than the Muni. And what if a case demanded I go out of town? How could I possibly do that and still maintain my independence?

I couldn't.

There must be a solution—and I would find it.

I got off the streetcar at Ninth Avenue and walked the two blocks to Piper's apartment building on Tenth.

The first thing I noticed was that the wheelchair ramp was gone. Strange: she still had occasional need for it. Then I saw that the front door was again off the latch. This wasn't a high-risk neighborhood, but the residents' security precautions seemed irresponsibly lax. I went in, crossed to Piper's door. It, too, was ajar. I moved through it.

Into an empty apartment.

No Chinese prints on the walls in the hallway. No furniture grouped around the gas-log fireplace. No dining table. Not even indentations where the furniture had stood on the carpet. The odor of fresh paint was in the air. I went to the kitchen and found the cabinets and refrigerator empty, the stove and oven shiny clean.

From there I moved to the closed door off the living room. A narrow bedroom, empty. The closet contained nothing. I checked the shelf, found only a wire hanger jammed into a far corner. The next door opened onto a bathroom with nothing in the over-the-sink medicine cabinet or linen storage. The last door led to what must have been Piper's office; multiple heavy-duty power outlets indicated so, but there was no sign of recent occupancy.

It was as if she'd never lived here.

Never existed.

I reached down to touch the carpet. Dry, but my fingers came away smelling sweet—a faint floral aroma. That explained the lack of indentations from the furniture: someone had recently done heavy-duty cleaning as well as painting here.

I began to prowl, looking for some trace of Piper.

But there was nothing except for the hanger in the closet.

It had been less than seventy-two hours since I'd seen her. This makeover had been clean, fast, and efficient. Why?

I went out to the vestibule and checked the mailboxes; no labels on any of them. Upstairs I rang the bell of the second-floor apartment. No reply there. Same on the third floor. I was somewhat winded from the climb, so I sat down on the top step and phoned the agency, asked for Adah, and explained the situation.

"Should I call the department?" I asked. "And if so, which detail?"

"Don't do that. You could be accused of trespassing. Besides, while this new chief has started to clean things up over there, they're still in what I call a state of disarray." The SFPD had been plagued for years by scandal, mismanagement, and dissension.

What Adah didn't have to remind me of was that when she had quit the department she'd been very outspoken to the press about conditions there. And her fellow officers had retaliated by shunning her. Any request from someone associated with her was not going to receive prompt and courteous attention.

"Adah, something's got to be done about this situation."

"I know. Stay put. I'll be there as soon as I can." Her voice sounded light and somewhat excited. Adah, like me, was addicted to tackling tough cases.

I put my phone away and went back into Piper's empty apartment for another look around.

ADAH JOSLYN

Damn! The entrance door to the Tenth Avenue apartment building that Shar had called her from was locked.

She buzzed the downstairs unit, got no reply. Where the hell was Shar?

As she was about to press the button for the second floor, a woman in running clothes opened the door and brushed past her. Going someplace in a hurry, and she didn't look back when Adah slipped inside.

Well, now I'm trespassing too.

The apartment door was closed, but unlocked. Adah opened it and moved along the hallway. The bare walls looked and smelled freshly painted. Nothing in any of the rooms that indicated recent occupancy. On the bedroom floor she found a single wire hanger—the kind dry cleaners used. She picked it up, examined it. There was a torn piece of label and a sticky substance on its neck. She suspected who had done the tearing.

Oh, Jesus, Shar! Why didn't you wait for me?

Adah sat down on the raised hearth of the living room fireplace, still fingering the hanger, thinking what to do next. Run out to every dry cleaner in the vicinity, hoping to catch up with Shar? Call Dom Rayborn, her replacement on the SFPD homicide detail, and the only person on the force she trusted?

What exactly would she say to him?

Dom, I'm in this empty apartment where there's no evidence of anybody living recently, but my boss claims a friend of hers was here on Friday.

Dom, I know this sounds crazy...

Dom, my boss may be in the clutches of a maniacal dry cleaner....

Yeah, right.

Well, then, back to the old well-practiced routine—canvass the neighbors.

"Be right there," a man's voice called out from the second-floor unit. Less than a minute later he opened the door—tall, wide, with a shiny bald dome fringed by buzz-cut gray hair. He stared at Adah.

She thought she knew why she'd surprised him: he'd probably expected someone else, and now he was confronted by an equally tall, slender black woman with intricately woven cornrows.

She showed him her credentials—no longer an SFPD shield, but the private investigator's license and McCone Agency card made her feel better than she had in years.

He looked steadily at her. Not one to be cowed by a semi-official ID.

"So whadda you want?"

"Your downstairs neighbor, Piper Quinn—"

"Who?"

"The young disabled woman—"

"There's nobody disabled in this building."

"Ah, Mr...."

He didn't supply his name.

"How long have you lived here?"

"A while."

"What's 'a while'?"

"None of your business."

Secretive sort, maybe paranoid. His eyes were jumpy; he kept moving to block her from looking inside the apartment.

"In all this 'while,' you've never met Piper Quinn?"

"No."

"Or noticed a wheelchair ramp on the front steps?"

"Absolutely not."

And now that Adah thought about it, there had been no marks on the steps to indicate there ever was a ramp.

Was Shar losing it? Creating an imaginary friend and problem?

No. Adah had known her far too long; she shouldn't've entertained the thought for a second. And as an investigator she sensed the falseness of the situation: the immaculate ready-to-rent appearance of the first-floor apartment; this man's too quick and firm denials; the focused look of the woman in running clothes who had rushed past her at the front door.

"Well, thank you," she said to the man, turning away. He nodded, shut the door.

She started up the stairway to the third floor, trying to recall the woman's features. But they were a blur.

There was no answer upstairs, but she hadn't expected one.

Professional job, she thought as she started down. Removal of the resident—willingly or unwillingly—and quick cleanup. Other residents either paid off to say Piper had never lived there or, more likely, involved in the abduction.

Witness protection folks? No, they stripped people of their belongings and identity, but they didn't try to make it look as if they'd never existed. Other government agency? Homeland? NSA? CIA? What sort of threat had Shar's friend held for national security? Private security firm? Possibly. Hy's RI had the capacity to mount such an operation.

She'd have to talk this over both with Craig and Hy. They were much more familiar with government agencies than she.

What about Shar? Well, she must be pursuing a lead connected with that hanger. Ted had been right: Adah had to get over this protective crap, and now was the time to start.

In the entryway, the front door slammed. Footsteps crossing the lobby floor, and coming up the stairway.

Shar?

Adah had reached the second floor landing when she encountered the woman in running clothes, a plastic dry cleaner's bag draped over her left arm. She had short gray hair, a hooked nose, and round, owlish glasses. Her legs and arms were well muscled, sinewy.

Adah said, "I'd like to ask you a few questions," and extended her card.

The woman ignored it. Without warning she dropped the dry cleaning bag and lunged at Adah, strong hands grasping her arms, pushing and then pinning her against the wall.

The suddenness of the attack surprised Adah enough so that she had no chance to use her police training skills. The woman twisted her into the railing, and for a moment she was afraid she might be flung over. She managed to catch hold of one of the posts, her spinal discs protesting as she struggled against the shoving weight. Unable to break free, she kicked out instead and her shoe connected solidly with her assailant's right knee.

The woman's leg buckled and she screamed, "Bitch!"

Above, a door opened and the man's voice called out, "Eva? You need any help down there?"

Adah managed to get both her hands inside the clutching fingers, but still couldn't pry them loose. Furiously the woman, Eva, whirled her around again and threw her against the wall. Slammed her head hard into the unyielding plaster.

The blow scrambled Adah's senses, weakened her struggles. The next thing she knew she was on the floor with Eva on top of her, both knees pinning her outthrust arms. Dimly through tears of pain, she saw the woman reach into the pouch pocket of her hoodie, withdraw her hand swiftly with something long and shiny in her fingers. Adah recognized the object just before it descended toward her upper arm.

Hypodermic needle.

No!

She fought wildly but she didn't have enough strength and it was already too late. She felt a painful prick in her upper arm—

And that was all she knew.

MICK SAVAGE

His fingers skipped over the keyboard in search of background on Specialist Ryan Middleton. There wasn't much information.

Born Portland, Oregon. Fifteen years older than Piper and, like her, no siblings, and both parents deceased.

Middleton had graduated high school in Portland, then earned a degree at Cal Poly in San Luis Obispo, majoring in electrical engineering. Had gone into the marine corps shortly after graduation. Married to Piper Quinn in San Francisco six years ago. Deployed to Iraq the next year.

A patriot? Or another victim of the poor job market?

Specialist. What kind?

Well, in Middleton's case, he had been a tactical intelligence officer, stationed in Mosul, the third largest city in northern Iraq and a stronghold for Al-Qaeda and other Sunni militants.

Middleton—nicknamed Middie—had been off duty and walking with two of his fellow officers in the city center when a suicide bomber's truck stopped and detonated nearby. He and his companions were killed in the explosion. Middleton's mangled body came home along with many other flag-draped coffins.

Mick closed his eyes, pictures of those coffins slowly coming off the military planes flashing through his mind. For a long time the previous administration had prohibited the press from photographing them; the ban—pending the deceased families' consent—had since been lifted, and rightly so.

Mick himself could've been in one of those coffins, except for a mild asthmatic condition that qualified him as 4-F.

That and a strong conviction not to serve in a war as wrong as any his country had ever undertaken.

He kept looking for further information on Ryan Middleton; nothing except a high-school yearbook photograph. It showed a nondescript, dark-haired kid with a prominent cowlick. His eyes were hooded, secretive, as if shielding himself from the probing lens. At Cal Poly he'd kept a low profile; he was not pictured in the yearbook with any clubs or other student organizations. His graduation photo was not very different than the one taken in his senior year of high school, except his hair was cut shorter, the cowlick not so prominent.

Mick composed a report and shot it over to Shar's computer. Then he started digging on the elusive Melinda Knowles.

CRAIG MORLAND

In spite of Thelia's thinly veiled warning to leave off the business about Shar not testifying in the Andersen appeal, he kept reviewing the file throughout what should've been his lunch hour.

Andersen Associates, headquartered in nearby San Jose, had been awarded a contract by the previous presidential administration to rebuild power plants in Kabul, Afghanistan. An investigation by a prominent Internet blogger, Josh Ramsey, had supposedly uncovered work undone and gross overbillings by the company. The suit went to trial and the government won. Andersen appealed, and hired McCone Investigations to provide supporting evidence.

Thelia's investigation had turned up significant links between Josh Ramsey and a major witness for the prosecution in the case, a CEO of a rival contractor who was vying with Andersen for a second, more lucrative job in the Middle East. Money had changed hands through a lobbyist who had no connection to either party.

Shar had then taken over the case, flying to the East Coast to interview the lobbyist. Nothing had come of that. The CEO of the rival contractor didn't return phone calls. Josh Ramsey, who lived in Seattle, was the weak link: he broke easily under questioning, gave a deposition, and would be testifying for Andersen in the appeal.

All of it clear-cut.

So why, Craig wondered, did he feel so uneasy about Shar's testimony?

There's nothing wrong with her memory or grasp of the facts, Craig.

But what about her emotional state?

When she'd come back to the agency on a limited basis in December, she'd been quick to anger. Of course, she'd always had a short fuse, but this was somehow different. One day he'd knocked and walked into her office, but apparently she hadn't heard him: she was hunched in the armchair under the fake plant, crying. Not one for crying women, he'd fled without her seeing him.

He should've stayed, tried to be a friend. All the things she'd done for him: giving him a job when he'd come west to be with Adah. Taking him down a peg when his stuffy, macho past experience threatened to control him. Bringing Adah on board when the alternative was for them to move to Denver, where the PD had offered Adah a lucrative desk job far from the people they knew and loved.

He thought of the things she'd done for others: keeping Rae Kelleher on as an assistant when Rae had been an emotional mess, supporting Mick through a difficult adolescence. Making allowances for Julia Rafael's checkered past. Hiring Patrick Neilan when he didn't really have the qualifications and sending him to a good lawyer when he wanted to sue for full custody after his junkie wife let a cokehead move in with her and their two boys. Taking a personal interest in training all the employees, and caring about their lives.

He remembered the Christmas dinners at Hy's and her house near the Glen Park district. The way she'd consoled Adah and him when their fat cat, Charley, had died. Even when she'd been in a locked-in state last year, she'd communicated with all of them with her wide, blinking eyes.

Generosity. Love.

And he couldn't even comfort her.

He'd always shrunk from emotional scenes, probably as a consequence of his staid upbringing. Raised voices, vindictive words, tears, objects hurled and destroyed—they'd had no place in the Morland family. Even when, much to their disappointment, he'd announced he was joining the FBI, neither his mother nor his father objected. It was a noble, patriotic calling—even if it wasn't the prestigious Big Eight accounting firm they'd hoped for.

Craig often entertained fantasies of taking Adah home to Alexandria as his bride. They'd marry here in California with her parents and their friends in attendance, then go east and totally shock his bigoted, Waspish parents. But he knew they'd eventually be won over by her beauty and infectious personality. Shit, they'd probably love her more than they'd ever loved him.

Not a bad scenario.

But repeatedly, Adah had said no. It had to be done right if it was to be done at all. Her parents loved and accepted him; she would not marry him till his parents felt the same way toward her.

Okay, he thought, tonight he'd pave the way. When he got home he'd e-mail them a photo of Adah and him.

TED SMALLEY

He frowned, contemplating the leaf from the fake ficus in Shar's office that he'd put on his desk to remind him to call around to nurseries for a living, breathing replacement. He'd gotten involved with other things and now it was after five and too late.

He took Shar's choice of a live plant as a sign of hope that she was returning to her vital, strong self. And she would have such a plant in her office by tomorrow afternoon. He'd get started on it first thing in the morning.

The pier was quiet, even though he knew others were still working. McCone Investigations occupied the entire upstairs of the north side, and the other businesses that had offices there were what he thought of as silent: architects, clothing designers, editorial services, an acupuncturist. The ringing of their phones was white noise, as were the voices and slamming of car doors at starting and quitting time. Now even that had passed.

Peace, blessed peace.

He began straightening his desk. He and Neal planned a quiet evening at home tonight. Neal's lasagna—he'd taken over the cooking when he closed his secondhand bookshop and become an online seller—and a remastered DVD of *Casablanca* that a friend had given them for Christmas. Domesticity—that suited them best.

Ted's early years in the city had been wild: multiple partners, gay bars, and bathhouses. Lucky he hadn't contracted
AIDS like so many others who'd indulged in a similar lifestyle.
While at All Souls, he'd lived in a small room with red-flocked
wallpaper, a fake tinned ceiling, and a loft bed shielded by sheer
curtains—a den for seductions that he'd decorated himself. But
then friends had started dying of that damn disease and he'd
become increasingly withdrawn. Most of his evenings had been
spent in the kitchen playing cards or board games with the others or watching old movies in the living room late at night with
Rae. When Shar moved the agency out of the big Bernal Heights
Victorian, he'd been happy to go along. By then he'd met Neal
and they were planning a life together. A life that worked, most of
the time.

But it wouldn't work if he didn't get his ass home.

He finished clearing the desk, stacking files and papers into
their appropriate places. And then, suddenly, he realized Shar
hadn't come back to the pier since late morning. Adah had rushed
down the stairs shortly after noon. She hadn't come back either.

His hands tensed on the desk edge. Adah he wasn't worried
about, but Shar...?

He called her cell. Out of service, or probably dead; she was
always forgetting to charge it. Dialed her house; only the machine
was home. Hy's cell and office number went to voice mail.

Okay, call Adah.

Out of service too.

At their apartment, Craig answered. "Adah's not here. I'm a little concerned. We'd planned to go to an early movie and then to
dinner."

"When did you last speak with her?"

"Um...not since we arrived at the agency this morning."

"Separate vehicles?"

"Sure. I never know when I'll be called out on something and I
don't want her to be stranded."

"She didn't tell you where she was going before she rushed out of here around noon?"

"No. I didn't see her."

"Well, I'm sure she's all right."

"Hope so. Why're you calling?"

He didn't want to cause Craig any more uneasiness. "Just a scheduling conflict. Will you ask her to give me a ring when she gets home?"

"Will do."

Ted hung up and swiveled to face the wall, where a poster from last year's ZAP Fesitval—zinfandel tasting—hung.

Shar unavailable. Adah late and also unavailable.

Not unusual, but he had a bad feeling about this.

SHARON McCONE

So that's the situation."

I sat across a table from Hy in Volpi's, our favorite neighbor-hood Italian restaurant. The lighted candle between us empha-sized the strong lines of his face, his thick mustache, and the gray streaks in his dark-blond hair. The streaks, I thought, made him even more handsome than when I'd met him. Handsome in a rough-hewn way. He'd aged well, the lines on his face showing equally the pain and joy he'd experienced in his life.

I, on the other hand, didn't want to look in the mirror. That stupid white skunk streak in my horrible cropped hair. Wrinkles that I hadn't possessed before I was shot.

I was seeing a handsome man, but what the hell was he seeing when he looked at me?

Just *me*, it seemed from the expression on his face when he reached for my hand across the table. Outward appearances weren't of great importance to Hy; he looked at the person inside.

He said, "You went rushing around so you wouldn't think about Allie. I know you're concerned about Piper, but..."

I shrugged. The cat's death was another in the long chain of losses I'd experienced since last July, and I didn't want to talk—or think—about any of them.

"So," Hy said after a moment, "the number on the dry cleaner tag was Piper's. Good work."

"Well, if anybody knows about dry cleaners, it's me."

He smiled. I'd often commented that I was putting the children of Mr. Omani, whose establishment was three blocks from us on Church Street, through college. Probably those of his employees too. I like silk and wool and pure cotton. They require special care and ironing, but my washer and dryer are old, and years ago, in a fit of rebellion against household chores, I gave my ironing board and iron to Goodwill.

"It's interesting," I said, "that a woman whose description matches Melinda Knowles's picked up a sweater and slacks belonging to Piper when the shop opened this morning. One more last-minute detail taken care of."

"Funny that a cleanup crew would miss the hanger that you found in the closet."

The waiter delivered our entrees—eggplant parmigiana. When he'd gone, I said, "It was wedged pretty far into the corner behind the shelf."

"Still, it's sloppy work."

"Cleanup crew. People who remove evidence at the scene of a crime. The government has them, all the big security outfits have them—including RI."

"Yeah. I'd like to tell you ours was used for good purposes in the past, but it wasn't always. Not till I took control."

RI, Ripinsky International, used to be known as RKI— Renshaw & Kessell International. Hy was originally a silent partner who undertook especially risky jobs, such as hostage negotiation. Then Dan Kessell had been killed and Gage Renshaw had made himself disappear, and through the partners' agreement Hy had become sole proprietor. He'd immediately set about ridding the company of the unsavory personnel and practices that had been prevalent during the Renshaw and Kessell years.

I could imagine what the cleanup crews might have had to deal with back then. It wasn't a pretty picture.

"Tell me exactly how these cleanups work."

"A situation comes up—somebody needs to disappear or, in the old days, is made to disappear—and there has to be a cover-up. We send the crew out. An unmarked delivery truck that bystanders might assume is a rental arrives, with five skilled people and all the equipment they need to erase the existence of the client or the victim on board. They go in and out within twelve hours. Nobody knows they've ever been there."

"They dispose of bodies?"

His mouth set in grim lines. "Not ours anymore. But yes, sometimes."

"What about in the case of a multiple-unit building like Piper's—how do they get around the other tenants?"

"They can be paid off. Or forcibly replaced. It happens. But here's a suggestion for you: check to see if all three apartments in Piper's building were rented, and if so, when. If this was a disappearance long in the planning, whoever engineered it may have moved in their people over a period of time."

"Good idea!" I couldn't wait to sit down at my laptop and get started.

"Slow down and eat your food, McCone. It's getting cold."

There were several messages from various family members on our machine when we got home. One, from Ma, sounded particularly distraught, so I called her back first. Her husband, Melvin Hunt, had been diagnosed with bladder cancer last summer and, after treatment, it had looked as if he was in remission; now symptoms had recurred and he'd been admitted to the hospital for tests. I offered to come to San Diego, but Ma said no, Charlene was closer and John was right over in the next town. After I confirmed that with them and left a message for Patsy—whose restaurant business kept her on the go—I logged on to the computer. It was better than sitting listening for the pad of Allie's paws on the hardwood floor.

Piper's building was owned by a corporation that had large

holdings in the Sunset. Managed by City Realty on Kirkham Street in the heart of the district. I went to their Web site and found two rental offerings at that address: the second- and third-floor apartments. There was no mention of the ground-floor unit Piper had occupied. It was as if, along with her, it had never existed.

I considered the apartment: long and narrow, its extra rooms taking up part of the garage. An illegal unit designed to generate under-the-table income? That was possible, but I didn't think Piper would've gone for it; she'd run a business from there, and needed to report rental expenses to the IRS.

So how had someone tampered with the property records?

Easy, in the age of skilled hackers.

Could Mick or Derek, with their forensic computer technology, figure out what had happened? No, to do that you needed access to the machine itself. Of course, with this new search engine they'd created, anything might be possible.

And Mick was only a phone call away.

MICK SAVAGE

Tonight? You want me to do this *tonight*?"

"Please." His aunt's voice could melt chocolate.

But, damn, he was in the middle of something. He'd met this woman—not in one of the clubs, but at Macy's, of all places, where he'd been buying new socks. Alison Lawton. She was also buying men's socks because they fit better on her size-ten feet. The feet were not a detraction.

Tall, willowy, long-haired blonde. Spectacular-looking, but nice, genuinely nice. And funny. She didn't think the less of him when he confided that all of his socks had holes in the toes or heels. He hadn't protested when she'd stopped him from buying the cheap on-sale ones.

They'd gone for a drink at Scala, off Union Square on Powell Street. She was a stockbroker with Merrill Lynch and was greatly relieved that the economy was turning around. Originally from farm country in Indiana, but now every inch the sophisticated West Coast urbanite. She called her well-tailored black suit and matching low-heeled pumps her "disguise."

"They can't get you when you blend in," she told him, "and black is definitely the way to do it."

They stayed at the restaurant for dinner, sharing more of the details of their lives. She'd won first prize in Junior Quilting at the state fair. He'd been a star running back at his high school in

Pacific Palisades—before he was suspended for hacking into the board of education's computer system. She'd gone to University of Wisconsin and majored in business and partying. He'd never gone to college and sort of wished he had. She'd been engaged once but broke it off—a nice guy, but boring. He'd lived with a woman whom he had thought was the love of his life, but no longer.

Now they were having coffee at his condo, a place where he'd never expected to entertain a woman again.

He mouthed, "My boss." To Shar he said, "Can't it wait till tomorrow?...But I've got a friend here....I know you're worried, but— Okay, I'll try."

He closed the phone, looked at Alison, who was smiling quizzically.

"She's a tyrant. She's my aunt and I love her, but she's a tyrant."

To his surprise, Alison retained her smile. "She can't be all that bad."

"Oh yes she can. She threatened to kill me when I was just a little kid."

"Why?"

"Because I wouldn't pick up my toys."

"Good for her."

"What?"

"I think I already like your aunt. I bet she would've made you buy new socks long before this."

He raised his hands in surrender. "Okay, you're telling me to get on with this crazy search of hers?"

"I am. And I'll let myself out. Tomorrow's a busy day."

He felt as if he would wilt on the spot.

"I'll call you in the afternoon," she added. "And dinner tomorrow night will be on me."

Call him? Dinner tomorrow?

You're back in the game, Savage. Don't screw up this time.

As the door closed behind Alison, Mick poured himself another cup of coffee and sat down at his workstation.

Apartment building on Tenth Avenue. Names of recent tenants. It was a no-brainer. He should've asked Alison to wait.

But an hour later he had to concede he was up against something that outstripped his considerable abilities. Up against something bigger than he'd ever contended with before.

ADAH JOSLYN

Her limbs were cramped and aching, the back of her head throbbed, and her nostrils were clogged with a strange odor. Dust and something else... what?

She breathed deeply. Dry-cleaning fluid. The same kind of stuff she stuck in the special bag with her sweaters and whirled in the dryer because it supposedly worked as well as the professional process, except that it didn't.

Where the hell was she? She remembered earlier thinking about Shar in hot pursuit of a maniacal dry cleaner. Ridiculous.

Darkness all around her. Small space—she could feel it. Surface on which she was lying probably carpeted. But why wouldn't her arms and legs work? She bent her fingers, felt her wrists.

Duct tape—that miraculous invention. She'd patched pipes, repaired furniture, even hemmed jeans with it. And now somebody had used it to truss her up.

"Shit!" she said. The word echoed hollowly around her.

"*Help!*" she yelled.

The effort made her head hurt even more and brought no response.

She listened for sounds. Only a heavy silence. Wherever she was, hollering wasn't going to attract any attention.

She wriggled around and arranged herself as comfortably as

possible—which wasn't very. So what had happened to her? She forced her sluggish mind to recall.

Okay, she'd been on the second-floor landing of a building—Shar's friend's building. And she'd met the large woman she'd earlier seen leaving. They'd fought, and the woman was incredibly strong and had battered her pretty well. Who was she?

Eva. That was the name the man in the apartment above had called down to her.

But who the hell were they? And why had Eva shot her up with the stuff in that goddamn hypodermic needle? And how had she gotten here—wherever *here* was?

Dry-cleaning fluid. She sniffed again. It wasn't on her clothes or in the air, it was in her system. Some chemicals, when injected, could cause such an odor.

Oh God, those drugs weren't easily available on the open market. As she'd suspected, she was dealing with pros here. But what kind of pros? And what did they want with her?

And Shar? Had they grabbed her too?

So damn many questions...

She needed to pee. She repressed the urge, focusing on trying to free herself. But she couldn't get any of the tape off. Her fingers were half numb and she tore two nails down to the quick.

Give it up, focus on the surroundings.

A roughly six-by-four-foot space with a thickish mat on the floor and a low ceiling. The walls were metal; she bumped her head against one and the hollow noise told her that. Storage locker, maybe. Where? In the garage of Piper Quinn's building? That would make sense. Keep her inside, out of sight of the neighbors, then dispose of her by car.

Dispose.

The word made her shudder.

It was totally dark in here. Probably dark outside too; she had that middle-of-the-night feeling. By now Craig would suspect something had gone wrong; she never stayed away from home this long without calling. He'd contact Shar, who would tell him about this building. Unless he *couldn't* contact her. Unless something had happened to her too.

Please let somebody come looking for me soon!

Her bladder felt as if it were going to burst. She forced her attention again to the events of the morning, tried to piece them into a coherent sequence.

The empty apartment. The man in the second-floor unit. The woman on the stairs who had attacked her. Why, when she couldn't have had any idea of Adah's identity? Or had she? The man on the second floor had her card, might have put in a quick call to the woman.

Popping noises—two of them—startled her. They were muted, though. Could've been a car backfiring outside.

Or gunshots.

She squirmed around, trying to find the best position to lie in while she continued to try to pick at the duct tape.

A door opened, then made a hissing sound as it closed—one of those pneumatic devices. Footsteps slapped on what sounded like concrete. Something rattled and clicked. Someone removed what must be a padlock from a hasp and pulled open the storage unit door. Fluorescent light momentarily blinded her.

Massive dark figure filling the open space. It leaned in over her, hands grabbed her and rolled her on her side. She felt a stick in her upper arm.

Oh God, not again!

From the point where the needle had gone in, she felt the drugs coursing through her blood. She willed herself to resist, but it did no good.

Just before she lost consciousness, she caught the faint but unmistakable odor of cordite coming from her captor's clothing.

HY RIPINSKY

Shar had gone to bed, taking her cellular with her in case Mick called back with the information she'd requested. After he was reasonably sure she was asleep, he went down there and silenced its ringer. Then he unplugged the bedroom extension of their land-line. She'd be furious at him for that, but she needed her rest.

Subterfuge. So it had come down to that.

He sighed and went back upstairs. Got an IPA from the fridge and sat down on the sofa in front of the fireplace. The house seemed empty without Allie, whom he'd buried early that morn-ing next to her brother, Ralph, under the pines at the far lot line. Buried her with Shar standing by.

She hadn't cried, only silently placed a few dried flowers on the grave and gone back to the house. And she hadn't mentioned Allie the entire evening or responded to his attempts to talk about the cat. That bothered him more than most things so far. His wife was a passionate woman: she loved fiercely, whether the target object of her emotions was human or animal, and she'd treasured Allie. He was afraid she'd channel this loss into finding out what hap-pened to Piper Quinn.

And that was just too damn risky.

Pro job, he'd thought the moment she'd told him what she'd found at Piper's apartment building that morning. Removal, maybe by a government agency or some organization with covert ties. He knew all about such actions, dating back to his time in post-Vietnam Southeast Asia. Orders were issued, people disappeared or died, and no one was held accountable.

And it had continued to the present day, sometimes more frequently, sometimes less, but always there—a ripple on the smooth surface of what people thought of as normality. Yes, the players were different from year to year, decade to decade, and the current administration had taken steps to curb abuses, but how could they curb something so elusive that they might not even have knowledge of its existence?

Shar had to give up on Piper. He'd explain. She'd listen.

Outwardly she would. But privately she'd dig and dig and then—

He put the scenarios of what might happen out of his mind. He'd control this situation somehow.

Yeah, right.

He needed distraction, so he made a call he'd been intending to all week, dialed the number of the manager at the ranch they owned in the high desert country near Tufa Lake. Everything was fine, Ramon Perez told him. The sheep had yeaned, and the little ones were prancing in their pasture. The horses were wintering well; Ramon had been doctoring Sharon's favorite, King, for a split hoof, but wasn't worried enough to have the vet come out.

"Do it anyway," Hy said. "Our cat died last night, and another loss is just what she doesn't need."

"Of course." Ramon's voice softened. "How is Sharon doing?"

They discussed her for a few minutes, Hy downplaying his discontent and fearfulness. Ramon had had troubles of his own—the loss of one niece and sister-in-law, and the near loss of his favorite niece, Amy. Amy was living with Ramon and his wife, Sara, now, had a decent job, and was filling out college applications, but Hy knew what a difficult balance she walked between drugged-out and promiscuous teenager and sober, responsible adult. Knew that Ramon worried about her every day of his life. No need to burden him with his own problems.

Of course, after they ended their conversation, he realized he hadn't fooled Ramon one bit. Probably wasn't fooling anybody else either.

The phone rang five minutes later. Craig Morland. Without preamble he asked, "Have you or Shar seen Adah?"

"Shar talked with her this morning." He related what she'd told him about calling Adah from Piper's apartment, then rushing off before Adah arrived there when she found the dry cleaner's tag on the hanger. "She's been calling her cell all day, but it's out of service."

"And Shar isn't worried about her?" Craig's voice had gone from anxious to deadly cold.

"Of course she is."

"Funny way of showing it. She hasn't called here at all."

"I'm sure she's—"

"Stuff it, Ripinsky. I don't know about you, but I'm getting fed up with everything being all about Shar. She wants something, we hop to deliver. She screws up, we pretend it doesn't matter. Lots of people get shot; lots of people almost die and have difficult recoveries. But come on, man...."

For a moment Hy couldn't respond. Then he said with forced calm, "I hear you. And you're right to be worried about Adah." He described the scene at the apartment and everything Shar had found out.

"Jesus Christ! Why didn't *you* call me?"

"I didn't know about it till this evening, and Shar assumed if Adah had found out anything she'd check in. And why didn't *you* think to let us know she was missing till"—he looked at his watch—"eleven-thirty?"

Pause. "Because Adah's not good at outlining her plans to me. She could've been working or with friends or at a movie. It wasn't till Ted called and said she hadn't come back to the pier that I sensed trouble."

"That damned independent-woman shit."

"Well, you and I aren't so communicative about our plans either. But, Ripinsky, this sounds serious. You know what I'm thinking?"

"I do." And now he'd changed his mind about staying out of whatever was going on. With Adah apparently missing, they were already in it, like it or not.

Craig said, "Let me get on to my contacts at the Bureau. Ask if this is government-related or if they've heard any buzz about it. And give me the address of that building where Adah was supposed to be going."

He did, and he heard scratching noises as Craig wrote it down.

"You heading over there?" he asked.

"Right away."

"Want company?"

"No need. Why don't you start checking with your contacts at other security firms?"

"Will do."

Hy hung up, then reached for his BlackBerry and speed-dialed the one man in the industry he trusted: Trent Curtis, owner of TXC Executive Protection. He was located on the East Coast, conveniently close to DC and, even though it was now well after midnight there, always available to Hy.

Curtis must've been working because his voice was clear and alert when he picked up.

Hy explained the situation and asked, "You have any idea who may have engineered this thing?"

A pause. "There's been some talk here about a lucrative contract being awarded to a Frisco firm by a very covert intelligence agency, and that people from the outfit were sent out to assist. The fact that there's any gossip at all leads me to believe that either the government op or someone at the firm itself was careless with information."

"Which leads me to believe they're vulnerable."

"Exactly. You want me to put out the nets, see if I can come up with a name?"

"If you would, I'd appreciate it."

"Done." Another pause. "Ripinsky, watch your back. No matter who ordered this, you'll be going up against very powerful people."

TUESDAY, FEBRUARY 10

CRAIG MORLAND

The night was cold when he stepped out of his SUV on Tenth Avenue. Clear and star-shot, but about as icy as it got during San Francisco winters. DC's climate was more moderate at this time of year, but the summers—so hot and muggy that you could see the moisture in the air. His new home suited him better. His new home, and Adah.

Where the *hell* was she?

This was a quiet neighborhood at quarter-past midnight. A few lights glowed behind closed curtains and blinds, but for the most part the residents must go to bed early. Middle-class homeowners mixed in with renters; places well cared for; deep lots with backyards; probably a fair number of children to play in them. It reminded Craig of the street in the Inner Richmond where Patrick Neilan lived with his two boys.

The address Hy had given him was totally dark except for a light that illuminated its number. He went to the door, noting the lack of names on the mailbox, and pressed one buzzer after the other. No response.

He stepped back and looked at the building. A narrow alley ran along the left side, opposite the garage. He turned to scan the street. No pedestrians, no faces at windows.

He wasn't armed; his gun and shoulder holster were in the safe at the pier. Briefly he'd thought of stopping by to get them; he had a carry permit, but the situation really didn't warrant a weapon, and there was too much chance of discharging it accidentally in a public place. Bad enough he was about to commit criminal trespass; the gun would only compound the situation for him and the agency.

He headed for the alley. Lights on in a back room next door, but no windows overlooking his position. A security spot high up near the other building's roofline cast rays into both backyards; in this one he glimpsed plastic outdoor furniture on a stone patio and raised beds that held the withered remnants of tomato plants. A stairway led up to the second and third stories, but apparently the first-floor resident—Piper, Shar's friend—would have had to come around on the path to use the garden. Given her disability, Craig doubted she had.

As he headed for the windows of the ground-floor apartment, he scanned the buildings behind and to the right. A tall bushy cedar screened part of the view from the next street, and the windows to the left were dark. Not much chance that anyone over there had seen anything unusual here, but it'd be worth checking out at an hour when the residents were receptive to talking.

New-looking white pleated shades covered the large window of the apartment. Craig tried to open the sliding panels, but they were secure. A second smaller window was to his left. The same type of shades hung to the sill. The window wasn't locked.

He slid it open a crack, heard empty silence and smelled the fresh paint and newly cleaned carpet. He pushed up and eased himself over the sill, dropped down, then took out the small flashlight he kept in a zipper pocket of his jacket.

Empty room, just as Hy said Shar had described it.

Craig moved to the wall and edged along it to the open door. Same kind of silence, made oppressive by the fresh paint and sickly sweet carpet-cleaner odors. He raised the flash. Nothing but another empty room, and a single wire hanger lying on the raised hearth—the hanger Shar had found the dry-cleaning tag on. The reason she'd rushed out of here without waiting for Adah.

He moved through the other silent rooms. No evidence of violence. No evidence of what had happened to Adah. He wondered if she'd even gotten inside the building. But she must have, because nothing else would have kept her away from home this long.

He went to the lobby and scaled the stairs to the third floor—farthest place first. Its door was unlocked. He checked the rooms. No evidence of recent occupancy, and vacuum tracks prominent on the floor. Down to the second-floor unit, which also was unlocked. This one had been cleaned and repainted like the one below. Craig went over it slowly, looking for any trace the cleanup crew might have missed.

On the far wall of the living room near the middle was a lumpy place that had obviously been patched. He trained his light on it, then took out his Swiss Army knife and dug at the spot. Spackle crumbled, and he cleared it out, found a hole the size and shape of a bullet.

Christ! Had Adah been shot?

No, dammit. Somebody had fired a gun into this wall, but it didn't have to have been aimed at Adah.

He was sweating heavily, so he sat down on the raised hearth. What to do? Call the SFPD? He was here illegally. He'd lose his license and compromise the whole agency.

But losing Adah would be much worse.

Make an anonymous call? The cops weren't going to come out without probable cause—and certainly not for one of their own who had embarrassed them all by speaking to the press when she quit to work for a private firm. There'd been a lot of hostility toward Adah; the only person who would deal with her there was Dom Rayborn, her replacement on Homicide—and Craig suspected he was simply grateful that she'd opened up a slot for him on the elite squad.

He could report Adah missing after the requisite seventy-two hours, but they'd give the case little attention and by then it might be too late. This was something the agency would have to deal with on their own—with the assistance of Hy and RI.

One more place to check: the garage. There must be an entrance to it off the building's foyer.

He went back downstairs, found the door, opened it, and shone his flash around once he was inside. Room for two cars, if one was small enough to fit in the space that was truncated by Piper's apartment. A set of three storage lockers on the rear wall. They were all empty, but a padlock on one hung open from the hasp. He examined the inside closely.

Wet spot on the bottom of the locker. He touched it and smelled his fingers. Urine.

Somebody had been locked in here—and recently. Adah?

He stuck his head inside and breathed deeply. Under the urine smell was another—perfume, a brand not sold in the United States that he'd brought home to her when a case took him to Hong Kong. How many chances that another woman who wore that same scent had also been in this building?

A more careful examination of the locker revealed no other traces of Adah. Still, he could imagine her imprisoned here, without bathroom facilities and probably without food and water. Bile rose in his throat, and rage filled him.

Out of there, back through Piper's apartment into the yard. As he dropped down from the window, there was movement in the shadows at the rear of the lot, behind the beds full of dead tomato plants. A dark, slender shape, crouching low, darting into the shadow at the fence line.

Immediately Craig gave chase, but it was dark at the border of the deep lot, and he lost sight of his quarry. Something banged, and he went the way of the sound.

A loose board hanging crooked from the fence. Footsteps

pounding on dirt beyond it. He pushed through, saw a narrow unpaved lane between the two rows of buildings. At its end a hunched figure turned to the left on Kirkham and was gone.

Craig ran to the end of the lane and looked both ways on the cross street, but there was no sign of anyone. He ran up the block to Ninth Avenue and looked both ways. No one. And no one on Eleventh. Lost him. He returned to Tenth, where he'd parked his vehicle.

He started it up and drove to Pier 24½, parking on the Embarcadero a way down from the pier's entrance, and walking there. When Shar had been shot, the tenants had fired the drunken security guard who'd been on duty that night and put in his place a woman from RI. No more key cards, no more automatic openers in the cars. Nobody allowed inside without being visually identified by Bonnie Smith.

She smiled at him through the bulletproof window beside the entry. Face round and brown and wrinkled from years in the sun. She'd been a glider pilot and a skydiver and had spent most of her life on beaches. Had only moved to the city and taken this job because her elderly mother was ill and needed her. By day, she tended to things at home; by night, she worked and a sister took over there.

Craig admired the hell out of her.

"If you're looking for Adah," Bonnie said, "she's not here."

"I know. Coming in anyway. Something I need to do in my office."

Bonnie buzzed him in, and he crossed the floor and went up the stairs to the catwalk.

Adah's office was empty. He checked for messages, accessed her computer files. Strictly routine.

He went to his own office, which he shared with Julia Rafael, an all-around operative currently on vacation in Hawaii with her older sister and young son. Made calls and woke up all the agency personnel, who snapped to attention when he told them Adah was missing. They'd be there ASAP for an emergency meeting.

Then he began going down his list of his contacts at the Bureau, leaving messages that he needed information about any covert operations in the Bay Area.

SHARON McCONE

Four-thirty in the morning but they were all assembled—Ted, Kendra, Patrick, Craig, Thelia, Mick, Derek, Hy. Missing were the vacationing Julia Rafael and Rae Kelleher, who freelanced for us but was currently on deadline for her next novel. They were bleary-eyed, bedheaded, chin stubbled, but attentive and determined.

God, what a great team I'd created!

Since he'd called the meeting, Craig chaired it, outlining the situation. Crisp, incisive, more in his FBI persona than that of the mellow man he'd become after moving to the city. Hiding his emotions behind a years-long professional facade. And with good reason.

"I've checked with my contacts in DC," he told them. "Those who have called back say they've heard that the business with Piper Quinn is a 'matter of national security.' That means nobody is getting any voluntary information. Period. But I've got people working on trying to pry it loose."

"What happened to our 'transparent' government?" Mick asked.

"If you believe that…" Thelia said.

"Hy?" Craig nodded to him.

I watched him closely. When he woke me for the meeting his anger had been controlled; it still was to the casual eye, but to me he seemed even more on edge, his hazel eyes sparking.

Angry with the situation but also with me, I knew. As I was angry with myself: I'd been thoughtless, left Adah out there in danger.

Hy said, "My best contact in the private security sector has heard that a firm here in the city was involved. The cleanup job was contracted out by a covert agency. My contact's looking into it."

"How long will that take?" Craig asked.

"He's supposed to get back to me by this afternoon, latest. I have my own short list of firms to look at—the ones who get down and dirty. My contact indicated that the agency is highly covert."

"Mine said the same—so secret that even the White House and Congress don't know about it. Could be a holdover from the last administration."

I felt a helplessness settle into my bones. How did people like us go up against an agency so clandestine that even the president didn't know it existed?

Craig said, "Shar?" His voice had a distinct edge to it.

I related what I knew, hearing the tentative sound of my voice. I avoided the others' eyes, focusing on the table. This was not me, and the silence that followed my last words was not them.

Craig, his voice icy, finally asked, "Why didn't you wait for her?"

"I was following a lead. I knew Adah could take over for me at the building."

"And after you followed up on that lead, why didn't you go back to the building and look for her?"

"I did. Maybe you misunderstood me. The building was locked, and no one would answer my rings. I called Adah's cell, got no answer; then I went to the rehab center and tried to get them to let me look at Piper's records, but they wouldn't. I kept calling Adah all afternoon, but she didn't answer her voice mail here at the pier and her cell was out of service."

"But you didn't call our apartment. Or me."

"I didn't think..." I lowered my head, rubbed my fingers over the grain of the old oak conference table. "I made a bad error in judgment."

It was a difficult admission—like most people, I hate to admit when I'm wrong—but I meant it. I'd screwed up, put my friend and employee in danger, and now she might be lost to me forever.

"Yes, you did," Craig told me. "A major error."

"Craig." Hy held up his hand, a warning signal.

"Well, it's true. Talk about being cavalier with a friend's well-being."

I continued to rub the table. I had nothing more to say. No rationalizations, no excuses.

Ted broke the tension. "So we need a plan. Ideas?"

Craig said, "I don't think we should call in the cops. They'll just tell us to file a report after she's been gone seventy-two hours."

"But she was one of their own."

"Emphasis on *was*. When Adah left the department and spoke to the press about what a mess it was over there, she—in their vernacular—broke blue. That's the ultimate betrayal of her fellow officers. I doubt there's anyone on the force who will lift a finger for her."

Mick said, "Maybe one—her replacement on Homicide, that Dom Rayborn."

"If we go to him, I'd have to admit to trespassing. Rayborn's as by-the-book as they come. He'd arrest me and report the agency to the DOC licensing bureau."

"What about the FBI?"

"They're already helping on an informal basis. I'd rather keep it that way."

Mick shrugged. "Well, you know how to deal with them."

"I say we follow our leads. Keep contacting people," Thelia said. "I'll start monitoring Adah's credit cards and bank accounts to see if there's been any activity."

They were talking as if I wasn't there. I was losing control of my own investigative team.

I said, "What about canvassing the neighbors over there? Somebody must've seen something."

Hy nodded, looked at Craig. "You can do that. Tenth Avenue, and the buildings overlooking on Ninth."

"Right. I'll be there as soon as their lights start coming on."

"Maybe wait a little longer. Most people're more responsive after they've had their first cup of coffee."

Shut out. Shut out of my own investigation.

Hy said, "The rest of you will stay here, get on your phones and computers. See what we can turn up."

As the others agreed and started moving, I continued to stare down at the table. Moving my fingers over and over the wood's grain, thinking of how my life as an investigator had begun at this table, and how it might be ending. Hy squeezed my shoulder on the way out, but I couldn't respond.

TED SMALLEY

He'd stayed in the conference room after the others dispersed and now sat silently next to Shar at the table. After five minutes her head was still bowed, her breath quick and shallow.

Finally she said, "You remember when this table was by the windows in All Souls's kitchen?" The kitchen of the Victorian in Bernal Heights that the law co-op had occupied.

"Yeah, I do."

"Board games, poker, celebrating when things went well and bucking each other up when they went badly?"

"Uh-huh." He slid his hand over and touched her arm. She didn't seem to notice.

"What we were doing seemed so cosmic then, but it wasn't really. Poverty law. Helping those who couldn't help themselves." She snorted. "Sliding-scale fees. Cheap divorces. Tenant-landlord disputes. Child support settlements. And I bet half the clients faked their financial status in order to take advantage of our services. What a crock."

Throwing away the good things in her past. Damn!

Ted said, "No it wasn't. We helped a lot of people. Some of them wouldn't have survived without our efforts. Remember Bobby Foster?" A kid whom Shar had saved from the gas chamber. "After he was released from prison he went back to school, eventually became a teacher."

"True, but still we were such innocents, thinking we could save the world. And then all that changed."

"The world changed."

"Yes, drastically. There was a shift in values, and along with the rest of the country, we got cynical and materialistic. Those slick new lawyers that we hired toward the end usurped the firm and ended up taking it downtown. Before that we were so...in it together. We lived each other's dreams, fought each other's battles. Now it's as if we don't have any dreams, and we're all separate, alone."

"No, that's not true. Look how this agency has pulled together to find Adah. Look how we pulled together to find out who shot you."

"Maybe that's the problem. Since I recovered I feel as if I'm trapped inside a bubble. I don't belong here anymore. I look out of the bubble, but I can't connect with anyone or anything. Not even Hy."

"You're connecting with me now."

"Everybody connects with the Grand Poobah." She smiled weakly. "But maybe that disconnect is why I didn't really think of Adah yesterday. If I had, it would've made all the difference."

He clasped her arm more tightly. "You admitted to making an error in judgment. Who hasn't?"

"I make a lot of those lately, Ted. There're times when I just... stall. I lose myself in memories of all that lost time. I still have flashbacks to the shooting."

"It's all natural."

"I know that; my neurosurgeon tells me that. But it's hard to explain, and people around here are starting to think I'm losing it. I've become a liability, and maybe I ought to take myself out of the game."

"Or take yourself back in."

She looked into his eyes, nodded and swallowed as if she were digesting the comment. Then she stood, picked up her briefcase from the table. "I'm going to catch some sleep."

"And after that?"

"I don't know what I'll do next."

CRAIG MORLAND

There was an air mattress stashed in the conference room closet and, after he'd called another two contacts, Craig set it up and tried to nap. There wasn't anything he could do to help Adah till it was time to canvass the neighbors on Tenth Avenue, and he wouldn't be much good at that unless he rested.

But he couldn't tune out the ugly pictures in his mind. Adah being overpowered by some shadowy person. Adah confined to that little storage locker. Adah being loaded into some sort of vehicle and taken away. Adah—

Don't go there.

Finally he got up and drove over to an all-night coffee shop on Judah, on the corner of Ninth Avenue. Sat in a window booth and nursed a cup of what must have been the last of yesterday's brew. The sky was dawn-gray and lights were coming on in nearby windows. He'd give it another half hour or so before ringing doorbells.

He watched a streetcar rumble by, going west toward the beach, totally empty. Another one passed going inbound, only a couple of passengers' heads visible. When you wanted to ride one of the things they were always jam-packed, but when you didn't...

In spite of the delays Shar kept on riding the Muni. She'd ridden the same line out here yesterday morning, gotten off at the stop outside, gone to that building, called Adah, and then left her to face whatever was going on there alone. He knew it was irrational to feel so angry with Shar; she'd had faith in Adah's ability to fend for herself. Probably he would've done the same. And, yes, she'd made a mistake in not calling him when she didn't hear from Adah, but again it was because of that belief in Adah's self-sufficiency.

The very fact that Adah hadn't coped with the situation made it even more serious.

The day was brightening now. Going to be cold and clear again. A woman in a wheelchair rolled up to the building on the opposite corner and waited for an automatic door to open. A man with a gym bag appeared, limping, and went in behind her. Craig narrowed his eyes and read the discreet letters on the facade: ALTA VISTA REHABILITATION. The place where Shar and Piper Quinn went.

"More coffee?"

He looked around. She was a different waitress from the one who had served him when he'd come in: fresh-faced, almost pretty, her uniform clean and crisp. The shifts must've changed while he sat there.

"Yes, please." There were no other customers in the shop. "May I talk with you before the morning rush starts?"

She smiled. "Morning rush? The only customers we get in here are what I call the Septuagenarians' Social Club. Nine o'clock's early for them. Tell you what, I'll join you." She filled his cup, went back to the counter, and returned with one of her own.

This coffee was freshly brewed, much better. He smiled in appreciation, slid his card across the table. The waitress's eyes widened as she looked at it, but she made no comment.

Craig said, "I'm interested in a woman who may have come in here occasionally. In her late twenties, long blonde hair, walks with difficulty. She attends therapy sessions at the place on the other corner."

"I know her. Piper, I think her name is. Comes in sometimes with a friend, older than her, black spiky hair with a white streak. What's she done?"

"Piper? Nothing. I'm trying to locate her for a relative."

"Well, she lives in the neighborhood. The other one doesn't; she's always waiting for the streetcar. Are you sure this Piper hasn't done something?"

"Why do you ask?"

"Another guy was in here yesterday afternoon around two o'clock, asking about her too. Said he was her brother, but I don't know. . . . He looked kind of rough, not at all like he'd be related to her."

"Can you describe him?"

She sipped her coffee, closed her eyes. "Dark brown medium-length hair, full dark brown beard. Wraparound sunglasses that he never took off. About six feet, slender, but muscled like he works out a lot. Dressed all in black. Oh—and he had a small crescent-shaped scar on his right cheek. Looked like an old one."

Craig had had extensive experience with witnesses who embroidered on what they'd actually seen, but to him this sounded like the real thing.

"You're very observant," he said.

"I'm an artist in my spare time—portraits, mainly."

"Could you do a sketch of him for me? I'd pay you."

"Pay for my work? It'd be the first time anybody has."

"A hundred dollars?"

"Wow. More than enough. I can have it for you this evening."

She wrote her name—Roxanne Cramer—and number on a napkin and passed it to him.

Time to canvass. Craig stood, dropped bills on the table for the coffee.

As an afterthought, he asked, "Did you tell the guy about the other woman who comes in with Piper?"

"Yeah, he wanted to know about her friends, in case he couldn't find her. I told him what the friend looked like and that I thought her name was Sharon. Suggested he ask at the rehab place."

Where, according to Shar, they weren't forthcoming with patient information. Thank God.

SHARON McCONE

I felt useless, so I left a message for Craig, saying I would help canvass Piper's neighbors. Then I started ringing doorbells at the house directly across from Piper's building. When no one answered, I proceeded south.

A twenty-ish woman in a dark blue suit: "I remember seeing a blonde woman in a wheelchair, but I can't say what building she lives in."

A disembodied voice behind a door: "Go away. I don't open up for strangers."

A grumpy-looking man in a paisley bathrobe, coming outside to get his paper: "For Christ's sake, lady, it's seven-thirty in the morning."

A distraught young mother with a screaming infant: "Does it look like this is a good time?"

A thirties-ish man with punked-up hair, seemingly stoned: "I been playing this club all night. Leave me alone."

Slamming doors and no answers. A couple of kids nearly knocking me over as they lurched outside under the burden of heavy backpacks.

Standard abuse for my profession.

A friendly, plump woman in her forties, hands dusted with flour: "I've said hello to that girl passing on the street. As far as I know, the second floor of that building's occupied—I've seen lights. But they've been trying to rent the top unit for months. I thought somebody might be moving in over the weekend. A van was pulled up there on Saturday.... It was white, no name on it or anything.... No, I didn't notice the license plate."

The cleanup crew, no doubt.

More door slamming. More lack of response to buzzers. I went back and started working my way north.

Detached house with a good view of Piper's apartment house. A slender, slightly balding man in sweats, leaning on a cane. I'd seen him at the rehab center. "Oh, you're Piper's friend," he said. "Come in. I'm Perry Lennon."

He led me to a living room that was cluttered with books and DVDs and CDs. Shoved a load of them off an armchair and motioned for me to sit. "I'm worried about her," he said before I could speak.

"Why?"

"She hasn't been to rehab for well over a week. And she moved out of the building on Saturday. At least I think she did, because a van was there for a long time. And her wheelchair ramp is gone." He paused, looking sheepish. "We weren't friends, not like the two of you, but I liked her and kind of looked out for her. If she was planning to move, she would've said good-bye."

"When she didn't come to rehab, did you check up on her?"

"No. If she thought I was...well, monitoring her activities, she would've been furious with me."

Stalker, or a man with an unrequited crush? I suspected the latter.

"I did try to walk past there, late last night after eleven," he added. "I'm an insomniac. My back—I injured it a year ago in a skiing accident—gives me a lot of pain, but I have to be careful with the meds because I have an addictive personality. So sometimes I go out for fresh air."

"You say you *tried* to walk past?"

"That's right. I was on the sidewalk in front and I thought I'd look down the alley, see if Piper's lights were on out back. But then the garage door went up and this van—a small one, not like the moving truck, with its windows all covered—backed out of there, going fast. I had to jump aside and almost fell down." His nostrils flared in outrage.

"What color van?"

"Gray."

"And the windows were covered with what?"

"It looked like sheets, ordinary white sheets."

"You notice the make or model?"

"An Econoline, at least five years old."

To my surprised look he added, "I've got a photographic memory. Details don't stay with me as long as they did when I was younger, but this was only yesterday."

"I don't suppose you remember the license plate number?"

"Of course I do—4XAS560."

CRAIG MORLAND

The woman at the first house he tried told him to get fucked.

The man at the second place threatened to call the cops.

A kid in a ground-floor apartment stuck out his tongue and gave him the finger. Another good reason not to have kids.

Although he and Adah had talked about getting married, they both were skeptical about having a family. They knew some delightful children, but being around Patrick's boys had made them wary of procreating. Patrick had two: Rocky and Roscoe, he called them, but they were only nicknames. Their real names were Evan and Curtis. They called him Rex. The three Rs, Patrick explained, was their way of bonding after his ugly custody battle with their mother. Maybe it was the upheaval of that year but, damn, those kids were contentious.

Craig kept canvassing. He wished his credentials brought him the instant, wary cooperation that his FBI shield had. Most people didn't even look at the card he presented. Others stared at it in weary bewilderment. It was too early to talk, they said. How could he expect them to remember anything at this hour?

But the time he had left to find Adah was running out.

A few of the neighbors knew Piper. Two had seen the cleanup van at the building on Saturday. One had seen a jogger—female—going in and out the past week or so. Another said a big bald man lived on the second floor, but he must've moved out because a moving van had been there sometime on the weekend. Everyone who saw the van agreed it was white, except for one woman who thought it might've been brown or gray or maybe beige....

At the far north end of the block he struck pay dirt of a sort. A man remembered seeing Adah's car parked across the street, slightly overhanging a driveway entrance on Monday afternoon. That evening it had been towed away, probably at the request of the residents whose access it had been infringing on.

Craig went back to his van and from his laptop accessed the number of the towing service the city contracted with. When he called, he found they didn't have the two-year-old white Prius. A private contractor, then, but there were dozens, so he called the office and asked Mick to check.

Back on the street. A few more buildings, but no results. Then again pay dirt: a man with a cane, name of Perry Lennon. He not only knew Piper from rehab, but also said Shar had been there questioning him.

The woman was finally getting her act together.

"How long ago was she here, Mr. Lennon?"

"Half an hour, tops."

And she'd gotten the jump on him.

"What did you tell her?"

"The license plate number of a van I saw leaving Piper's building late last night."

By now, Craig thought as he got back into his SUV, Shar would have run the plate number through her contact at the DMV and be chasing down its owner. DMV information, while not so tightly guarded as Social Security numbers, was hard to get unless you knew someone who had legitimate access to the information, or someone who worked there, as Shar did. He himself had never developed a relationship with anyone at the DMV, relying on either her or Adah to get him what he needed.

He tried Shar's cell. Busy. Damn, he'd've liked to get in on this with her, but she was a good investigator and had half an hour's head start. Better for him to keep on canvassing.

SHARON McCONE

I walked from the streetcar stop toward the pier, then stood on the sidewalk breathing the cold, briny air. The day was winter clear, the kind that brings objects in the distance into sharp relief. I went to the chain-link fence between the pier and the fireboat station and looked across the water at the East Bay: I could see the buildings of downtown Oakland and houses high in the hills; for a change there was no smog or haze.

I'd lived in Berkeley for four and a half years while earning my BA in sociology. The degree had turned out to be useless in the job market of that time, but I was proud of it; my diploma hung on the wall of my office, along with citations and awards I'd never dreamed I would earn. I seldom returned to Berkeley, though, except to visit my half sister, Robin Blackhawk, who was attending law school there; she and I had become close after I discovered I was adopted and had a whole second family. But Berkeley's culture had changed, and my old friends were scattered. There were some things I missed: Telegraph Avenue and Cody's Bookstore; lazy afternoons at the Bier Garten; the quiet of the library and the noisiness at Sather Gate. But Cody's and the Garten were gone now, I had no need of the library, and if I walked by the gate or through campus I felt melancholy because my old haunts were now peopled by strangers....

My phone rang. My contact at the DMV, calling with the

information on the old van that had nearly run Perry Lennon over while backing out of the garage of Piper's building on Monday night. It was registered to a J. T. Verke, with an address in Cupertino, south in Silicon Valley.

My often-battered spirits soared, then just as quickly fell. I couldn't drive. How the hell was I going to get down to the South Bay and run a surveillance?

Then I recalled a conversation I'd had with my teenaged neighbor, Michelle Curley, last evening when I returned home and found her slumped despondently on my front steps. Despondence wasn't normal for Chelle: she had a cheerful, tough, in-your-face approach to life that complemented her spiky varicolored hair, multiple piercings, and tattoos. She'd graduated six months early from high school, and was taking business administration classes at SF State at night, waitressing by day, and saving her money to purchase dilapidated residential property to rehab and resell. I was certain she'd be a real-estate mogul by twenty-five, if not sooner.

"Mom told me about Allie," she said. In addition to her other enterprises, she house- and cat-sat for us, and loved the animals as much as we did.

I went up the steps and sat down beside her.

"I'm so sorry," she added.

"Thank you. She hadn't been doing well since Ralph died."

"I know."

"Aren't you supposed to be waitressing or at class?"

She slumped even more. "No class till seven. And my job got outsourced—to the owner's new slut. Just when I had almost enough money to buy that shack on Chenery Street. I could still swing it with help from my dad, but I don't want to ask him. I really want to do it on my own."

"You have an option on the property, right?"

"Yeah, but it's due to expire next month."

"How much more d'you need?"

"A thousand bucks." She smiled crookedly. "Doesn't sound like a lot, but without my job, it might as well be a million. And then I can't just let the house sit there; I've got to get the cash together for the renovations."

"How about a bank loan?"

She shook her head. "No bank's going to hand money to somebody with no job or prospects."

"True. You've still got your job with us, though."

"Shar, house-sitting for you—even when the cats were alive— isn't very lucrative. And don't you dare offer me a raise. I'm overpaid as it is."

Proud, tough young woman. She had what it took to succeed, if only life would cut her a break. I wished I had a magical solution.

Now, as I stood in front of the pier, a temporary one occurred to me.

I called her on her cell. She answered listlessly.

"No prospects on the job market yet?" I asked.

"You kidding?"

"Chelle, are you eighteen?"

"Last week, Tuesday. Why?"

"Sorry I forgot your birthday."

"No big deal."

"So this means your driver's license isn't provisional anymore." Meaning she could drive without a licensed adult in the car and, better yet, be paid to do so.

"Yep. Not that it matters; I don't get much use of the family car. Besides, it's a standard transmission, and I learned on an automatic."

"Well, my car is a stick, but I know of an automatic I can borrow, and I have an idea that will benefit both of us."

MICK SAVAGE

He was worried about Adah. She was like a sister—strange, because he had four of his own, and who needed one more? But he *was* upset: his morning's searches had all come up negative. None of the towing companies had the white Prius; there were no rental records for Piper's building; he'd found little more information on the dead husband, Ryan Middleton, and none at all on Melinda Knowles.

Mick didn't know what to do now, so he went down the Embarcadero to Miranda's, a favorite waterfront diner that had fallen on hard times but still claimed his loyalty, and wolfed down a giant cheeseburger and fries and two beers. As he paid the check, he belatedly remembered his dinner date with Alison Lawton that night. God, he hoped she didn't intend on eating early!

He was also worried about Shar. She'd looked so down when the staff meeting broke up. And she hadn't been in the office all morning. He called there, and Ted said she still hadn't come in; he called her cell and got voice mail; same at her house. But he knew his aunt: she was either out and about, working hard on the investigation, or—as had too often been the case recently—licking her wounds in private. Since she couldn't yet drive, that private place was most likely home.

He'd ride over there and check on her.

No one answered his ring at the house on Church Street. He pounded on the door, peered through the front windows, went around the back and looked through the glass doors off the deck. Nothing. Finally he checked out the garage.

Shar's vintage red MG wasn't there.

Why? She wouldn't have gone out and driven someplace—or would she?

Under normal circumstances, no. She knew that breaking the prohibition on driving till July could result in permanent loss of her license. But the Shar that he'd dealt with recently was not the one he'd known all his life. She'd always been a risk taker, but she calculated the odds. Lately...well, some of her actions didn't make much sense.

This thing about not asking for rides and taking buses everywhere—it was like that old David Janssen TV series *Harry O*, where the detective's car was usually in the shop and he rode around San Diego on public transit—some neat trick, since the MTS was inefficient and expensive. Or Janssen's other TV show, *The Fugitive*, his Richard Kimble had had better luck than his Harry O—there was always a bus coming along when he needed one, even on dark country lanes.

Well, like Harry O, Shar must've gotten tired of the whole stand-and-wait routine and decided to drive.

But to where? And for what purpose?

Suddenly Mick was afraid for her.

He decided to drop in at his dad's house in Sea Cliff, ask him and Rae if they'd seen her.

"No," Rae said. "Not this week. You?" she asked Ricky.

They were sitting on the overstuffed couch in front of the pit fireplace in the living room, their backs turned to the fog that was suddenly blowing past their house and through the Golden Gate to the north.

Ricky shook his head. "Shar doesn't stop by as often as she used to. Of course, given her mania for using the Muni, it's no wonder. She'd have to take the Geary bus, then walk for blocks."

Mick took a sip from the glass of wine they'd given him. Rae looked good, her red curls falling to her shoulders. A little tired, maybe; she'd said she was working practically nonstop on her novel.

Her novel. She'd always wanted to write what she called "shop and fuck" books, but while she'd been trying to do that, she'd written a beautiful novel with crime elements called *Blue Lonesome*. Drawing on her investigative background, she'd gone on to write two more equally well received novels, and was on deadline for her fourth.

His dad, a country-and-western superstar, had given up performing except for charity appearances and was now content to issue the occasional album and manage his recording company. He was, Mick thought, as handsome as ever, especially now that he'd stopped trying to cover up the gray in his chestnut hair. Mick, who looked a lot like Ricky except that his hair was blond, hoped he'd age as well.

He hadn't told them about Adah being missing. Confidential agency business. Anyway, he didn't want to talk to anybody about it, didn't even want to think about what might've happened to her. She'd be okay—he had to believe that, and it was enough for now.

"This mania for the Muni," he said. "What do you guys think of it?"

Rae shrugged. "An attempt at regaining her independence. All that time in a locked-in state, and then more in therapy. It must feel good to fend for herself, even if it's inconvenient."

"D'you think she'd do something stupid—like drive before her license is reinstated?" He explained about Shar and the MG being absent from her house.

"No," they both said in unison.

"Maybe the MG's being serviced," Rae said. "Or in storage."

"Or she's gotten rid of it and is planning on buying a new car," his dad added. "That vehicle is a dinosaur. And much too recognizable for someone in her line of work."

Mick shook his head. "She loves it, though, and she's kept it up beautifully. She's had big-buck offers for it, but she's turned them all down. I think she would've mentioned selling it."

"Well, I hope she did. I wouldn't want Red driving around in something that unreliable."

Rae—Red, to Ricky—elbowed him. "For me, he buys a new car nearly every year. But him, he still drives around in that old Porsche with the COBWEBS license plate."

Mick smiled. "Cobwebs in the Attic of My Mind" had been his dad's first big hit. He'd bought the navy blue Porsche with some of the proceeds, and Mick had insisted Ricky get personalized plates in honor of the song.

His cell rang. Alison Lawton. "We still on for tonight?" she asked.

"Sure. What time and where?"

"You know the Millennium Tower, Beale and Mission?"

"Yes." Of course he did: a sixty-story, blue-glass condo development near the Transbay Terminal. Its amenities included a five-star restaurant, state-of-the-art fitness center, and round-the-clock services.

"I'm on the twenty-fifth floor. The concierge will point the way."

They agreed on the time—seven—and Mick hung up, feeling a little stunned. "She's rich," he said.

"What?" his dad asked.

"This woman I met last night. She lives in the Millennium Tower."

Amusement sparked in his dad's and Rae's eyes. Mick had been born poor but raised rich and was about to become a millionaire in his own right.

"Okay," he said. "I know what you're thinking. But she didn't seem rich—just nice and funny and interesting. That's not a combination I run across every time I'm buying socks."

Rae poured him some more wine and leaned forward. "So tell us about her—and the socks."

TED SMALLEY

He wedged Shar's old MG into the last empty parking space on Telegraph Hill's Plum Alley. It didn't fit as easily as his Smart car, but it wasn't bad. No wonder she'd kept it all these years of living in the city, where space to tuck your vehicle was at a premium.

His building was an Art Deco classic that had been used as a location in the Bogart-Bacall film *Dark Passage*. Ted loved living in a place built in what he considered his favorite twentieth-century era. Maybe he should tap into the styles of that time for his next fashion statement—smoking jackets, hats, suits nipped in at the waist. No, his waist was testimony to Neal's great cooking; it would never be nipped in again. Silk was the answer, and he'd already ordered two shirts from Op Cit, the place where Derek bought his.

The elevator in its glass-block enclosure took a long time coming down to the courtyard. While well maintained, it was old and required patience. "That's my girl," he said as he pushed the Up button. The grate closed promptly and smoothly, as if the elevator appreciated his affection.

His apartment—two stories with sweeping vistas—echoed with silence. Neal had left this morning for the Pacific Northwest to buy a small collection for his online book business. Thank God there was enough lasagna left over for dinner. Ted hated to cook for one. He went up the spiral staircase to the second floor and took the bridge over the living room to the master bedroom. Changed to sweats, went back down, and opened a bottle of chardonnay—Deer Hill, Shar's favorite.

Then he sat down on the sofa. And fretted.

He was beginning to regret loaning the Smart car to his boss. She'd claimed she needed it because it was less conspicuous than the MG, but he knew that that wasn't true. For one thing, like the MG, the car was red. And while there were now plenty of Smart cars in the Bay Area, they still drew attention for their small size and maneuverability.

It wasn't until they'd exchanged keys and she left that he remembered she shouldn't be driving at all.

He sipped wine, considered the day. Adah missing, and still no word on that except the prospects for her survival looked grim. When people disappeared, hope diminished after the first twenty-four hours, and she'd been gone almost that long before anybody realized.

Years ago when Ted had met Adah at a dinner at Shar's house, they'd connected right away. And within months they'd bonded for life. Like her, he'd experienced prejudice. Like her, he'd known deprivation of the rights that were automatically granted to others. But unlike her, he hadn't been picked out of the mob of minorities, elevated and lionized by the SFPD for what she was, not *who* she was. For years she'd joked about being their "poster girl," but she was a damn good investigator and he knew how deeply the jibes from her fellow officers had cut.

Adah. Jesus, they couldn't lose her.

So here he was, exalted Grand Poobah of McCone Investigations, but in reality a mere office manager who'd often fancied himself an armchair detective—even though most of their cases baffled the hell out of him. In recent years he'd given up the pipe dream, but there was no better reason than Adah's disappearance to try again. He thought of Patrick's flow charts: logical placement of the facts of an investigation into a timeline. Maybe if he made a list...

He fetched his laptop and began.

#1 *Adah taken by a security firm hired by the same government agency that removed Piper Quinn for "reasons of national security."*
   Which agency?
   Which security firm?
#2 *Why national security?*
   Something to do with her dead husband?
   Something she'd seen around her building that she wasn't supposed to see?
   What about that bullet hole Craig found in the second-floor apartment?
#3 *Who was the woman in the apartment when Shar visited— the one who claimed to be Piper's aunt? Searches showed she didn't exist, but she had to, somewhere in some guise.*
#4 *Piper a drug user? McCone says unlikely, but how much does she really know about her?*
#5 *That security contractor. Need to ask Ripinsky if his contact has provided more info.*
#6 *Snatched by a stranger, a predator.*
   Why would a strong woman like Adah fall prey? More street-wise than that, unless taken completely off guard.
   Why would a predator lurk around that particular building? Why Adah, and not someone else?
#7 *Off pursuing a lead.*
   Too considerate not to check in.
   Unless a very compelling lead. No, would at least have called Craig.
#8 *Voluntary disappearance.*
   Trouble in the relationship? Who knows?
   Trouble on the job? She wasn't getting the action she used to

on the SFPD homicide detail, but she didn't seem to mind. Born administrator.

  #9 Dead or alive?

  Don't want to go there.

#10 Alien abduction.

  Contact Fox Mulder, FBI X-Files, Washington, DC.

Comic relief, after the previous question, but it didn't work. He deleted the point; he'd present the others to Shar tomorrow.

Odd, though: where had Shar gone after she left the pier this afternoon? She hadn't been forthcoming about why she needed something less conspicuous than the MG. Was she working on something she hadn't disclosed to the others?

Well, the agency files—except for very sensitive ones—were all open to him.

The armchair detective's fingers moved nimbly across his keyboard.

CRAIG MORLAND

The woman from the coffee shop on Judah, Roxanne Cramer, couldn't meet him with her sketch of the man who'd been inquiring about Piper until eight o'clock so, except for a trip home to feed the cats and grab a bite to eat, he spent the interim hours canvassing the buildings on the street behind Piper's, as well as those where there had been no response earlier. People were definitely more welcoming at the end of the day, and he came away with bits and pieces of information.

A woman across the street had seen a man "casing" the building on Sunday. She couldn't describe him accurately, except he was thin and bearded, wearing all black. Probably "one of those foreigners." What foreigners? Craig had asked. "Well, one of those that go around blowing things up—you know."

A man in the building directly behind Piper's had thought he saw a light moving inside her apartment on Sunday night. No, not after midnight, around ten o'clock.

So maybe somebody had been there before Craig.

The woman next door to the man had been awakened after midnight by the sound of running footsteps on the dirt path between the lots. She hadn't looked outside because "these days, the less you know, the better."

A dark, rundown house down the block appeared to be occupied by squatters. Craig avoided it: crackheads and derelicts made poor witnesses.

Another neighbor on Tenth Avenue described a muscular woman in a jogging outfit coming and going for the past week or so; she wasn't at all friendly and probably new to the neighborhood. No, the woman hadn't been around since the previous Friday.

A teenaged boy across the street had known Piper to say hello to, and he'd seen lights in the second-story apartment a few times.

Several people said they'd heard what could have been gunshots late Monday night, but they couldn't be sure. When Craig pressed them, they all admitted they couldn't tell the difference between a gunshot and a car backfiring.

The neighbors to the right of Piper's building had just gotten back from a two-week vacation in Mexico; they knew nothing of what had been going on. The house to the left was occupied by a young woman who said she was only house tending for a friend and feeding the cats twice a day. She'd noticed nothing.

There were the usual suggestions of satanic rituals and alien abductions, and a self-proclaimed psychic offered to tell him for a hundred dollars about the bad vibes she'd felt in the neighborhood.

By quarter to eight, he was seated at the bar in the Little Shamrock, a venerable pub on Lincoln Avenue across from Golden Gate Park. Drinkers gathered at the bar shoulder to shoulder, or lounged on the comfortable old furnishings. A noisy darts game was going on at the rear.

A pint of Guinness cleared his head of the jumbled voices of the people he'd talked with all day, but did nothing to ease his anxiety—or had it now reached the level of despair?—over Adah. While canvassing he'd relied on strict professionalism, going through the motions as calmly as if he were on a routine case. Now he could feel himself crumbling around the edges, and if Roxanne

Cramer didn't show up with the promised sketch, he might lose it altogether.

And then she was there, touching him on the shoulder and motioning to the bartender. Carrying both their pints, he followed her to a sofa near the front windows where, surprisingly, it was relatively quiet. When he sat, he smelled dust from the ancient velvet upholstery.

"I'm sorry I couldn't meet with you earlier," she said. "I started your sketch this afternoon, but I had a few interruptions and I wanted to get it right."

From her tote bag she took a sketch pad and flipped it open. "This is an honest-to-God likeness. I'd testify to it in court." She tore it off, handed it to Craig.

He studied the sketch in the dim light of the overhanging fake Tiffany lamp. It was good, detailed down to the way the hairs curled in the man's beard. The crescent-shaped scar on his cheek was small, but gave his entire face an evil cast.

"Roxanne, this is great." He pulled out his wallet, placed bills in her hand.

"My first paying job," she said. Then her eyes narrowed. "But this isn't just a job for you, is it? It's personal."

"Right."

"Well, I meant it about testifying in court. And I've got all your numbers. If the guy shows at the coffee shop again, I'll try to keep him there and call you."

"You don't want to take that risk. Look at him." He gestured at the sketch.

"Yeah, I know. He's dangerous. I'll watch myself." She stood, held out her hand to Craig, said, "Good luck."

And then she was gone, leaving him with the image of a man he'd never seen in his life. Time to put it out there and find someone who knew who the hell he was.

ADAH JOSLYN

That dry-cleaning odor was in her nostrils again. She moved, and a sudden spark of pain brought a moan out of her. She realized then that she was unbound and lying on a soft surface that might have been a feather bed. She smelled foul, her head ached, her muscles throbbed.

Darkness all around. Night, or a room without windows? A persistent creaking came from somewhere, but she couldn't pinpoint its source. A dripping sound too. The air was dank and stuffy.

She was still under the drug's influence. But she was alive—for now.

What time was it? What day? It had been morning, she assumed, when she'd been injected again in the garage storage unit on Tenth Avenue. They'd moved her, but to where and how long ago? And why was she no longer bound?

She pushed up, wincing and stretching out her long, cramped limbs. Turned around and walked straight into a wall. When she'd recovered from the shock, she felt its surface. Paneling. When she rapped on it a slight clanging told her the paneling covered metal. Another storage unit? No. The space was larger than that.

She put out her arms and, taking what as a kid she'd called baby steps, began to measure the size of the enclosure. Maybe six by eight feet, and no windows. A door, closed, and the knob didn't turn; it was on a snap lock and also secured by a dead bolt. But here on the opposite wall was an open door.

She felt her way through, ran her hands over the walls just inside. No light switch. She moved forward, banging her knee on something hard and unyielding. Ran her hands over it. A toilet.

She was in a bathroom. Blindly she felt around, found a sink, and then a tiny shower enclosure. And between them, a light switch.

She flipped it, and a dim bulb above the sink came on. There was no mirror. And it was just as well there wasn't. She didn't want to see what she looked like. After she used the toilet and drank some metallic-tasting water from the tap—allowing herself only a small sip at a time—she considered a shower in the stall that had been stripped of its glass door, but quickly discarded the idea; if her captors were close by, she didn't want to confront them naked. She cleaned up as best she could at the sink, using her shirt as a towel. Then she began hunting for a means of escape.

Toilet paper roll—plastic and of no use. P-trap under sink—corroded and unmovable without tools. Toilet guts—old and looked as if they might snap under pressure. Light fixture—nothing but a bare bulb, and she needed it to be functional.

Frustrated, she returned to the other room and rattled the doorknob. Listened for sounds outside, but all she heard was the creaking and steady dripping. It didn't come from any of the bathroom fixtures but from somewhere above.

Finally she flopped down on what the dim light from the door revealed to be an air mattress covered by a dirty comforter. The space contained nothing else. She drew up her knees, cradled her head on them.

Craig.

By now he'd be seriously alarmed. But, knowing her man as she did, he'd kept his head and been in contact with all his sources. The others at the agency and Hy would have too. They'd probably called in the cops and the FBI. All she had to do was hang on.

So how did you do that? She'd been in a kidnap situation before, but at least that time she'd known her captor and his motivations. It was the current lack of knowledge about what was going on here that frustrated her.

Her eyes felt moist as she thought of home: the spacious apartment in a Spanish-style building in the Marina. Their tortoiseshell cats, One and Other—they'd never gotten around to properly naming them—who ran eagerly to the door each time she returned. The rituals that had bonded Craig and her as a couple: FBI Fridays, when they watched DVDs of the old TV show and laughed at its largely false depiction of the Bureau; elaborate Sunday-morning brunches on the deck; silly voice and text messages that provided a lift during their busy days.

And then she thought of her folks. Had Craig told them she was missing yet?

Barbara and Rupert Joslyn. A mixed marriage: she, a college-educated, idealistic Jew; he, a working-class, pragmatic black. Still hale and hearty, still living in the old house on Powhattan in Bernal Heights. Disillusioned with communism, retired from radical rabble-rousing, but active in any number of liberal causes. Dad liked to tend his year-round vegetable garden and do intricate crossword puzzles. Mom liked to quilt and cook. She and Craig were supposed to go there for dinner on Sunday—

She felt a tightening in her chest.

Concentrate. Stay off the personal.

In reality she was much better off than Shar had been in that locked-in state last year. *She* had been unable to move or speak; for a time it had seemed certain she'd die. But there was always the possibility Adah could identify or even overpower her captors when they returned to do whatever they had planned for her. Or else try to bargain her way out of the situation, not that she had much to bargain with.

Or did she? They'd imprisoned her for a reason. Once they'd told her what they wanted and made their demands, she could comply with them or manipulate things in her favor. She just had to keep her wits about her.

That dripping—what was it?

Not rain—it was too regular for that. A slow leak in a pipe or downspout? Maybe.

And the creaking—it had stopped. Or maybe it had only been her imagination.

Adah's stomach rumbled. She couldn't remember when she'd last eaten. Oh, yeah, a deviled egg the morning she'd been snatched—another of Craig's and her crazy habits. They made a dozen deviled eggs on Sunday, kept them in the fridge for weekday breakfasts. There'd be a lot of eggs left over this week—

Stop that!

Drip, drip, drip...

SHARON McCONE

There's the address I want," I said to Chelle.

"It's dark."

"Yes. Park down here—there's a space."

"Okay." She sounded anxious. She'd readily agreed to the driving job, and had laughed as she'd clashed gears and lurched and stalled my MG on the trip to the pier for Ted's Smart car. But I'd felt her tension all the way to the South Bay.

"What now?" she asked as she pulled into the space.

"We wait a while to see if anybody comes or goes. If not, I'll go down there and check it out."

"Isn't that dangerous?"

"There's nothing to worry about," I told her. "This place belongs to a potential witness."

"Then why don't you just go up and knock on the door?"

"I like to size up situations first. Besides, I'm still waiting on that call back from Derek."

We sat in silence for around five minutes. I could almost hear Chelle's thoughts: irrational behavior. Why not act straightforwardly? Go and get what you came for. No bullshitting.

She would never understand the subtleties of investigation. But she'd make one hell of a businesswoman.

This was a quiet residential street in Cupertino, a suburb of San Jose, some forty-five miles south of the city. The neighborhood here hadn't caught up with the rest of Silicon Valley; the homes were small, dating from the seventies or early eighties and set on tiny lots. Windows glowed through poorly hung blinds or, in some cases, sheets. Television sounds emanated through too thin walls. In the porch lights I could see peeling paint and dead lawns and a few clunker cars up on blocks. Mostly cheap rentals, I guessed, or homes whose values had so decreased in the recession that their owners had ceased to care about keeping them up. It was close to seven o'clock, but only the occasional vehicle passed by; nobody arrived at or left any of the dwellings.

Chelle began tapping her fingers on the steering wheel. "This is boring."

"A lot of detective work is boring. You wait for information, you wait for people, you wait for something to happen."

"I don't think I'd be very good at it. I'm a results-oriented person."

"Results are the payoff in this business. When you finally get them—"

My cell vibrated. Derek.

"This J. T. Verke," he said, "owns the house in Cupertino outright. A Selena Verke pays the property taxes, and there's a document on file for dissolution of marriage in Santa Clara County five years ago. I'm currently running a search for another address for Verke in the Bay Area; it's not a common name, but there're likely to be some. Anything you want me to index it to?"

"Try security work—government or private sector."

"Right."

I broke the connection and turned to Chelle. "Okay, I'm going up there to the house. You have your cell, I have mine. Call me at any time; I'll answer. And lock the car doors."

"Are you sure it isn't dangerous?"

"Depends on how you feel about ex-wives."

That made her laugh—a tinny sound edged with relief. Immediately after I got out, the locks clicked.

I wondered if my employing Chelle as my driver was a mistake, even though her parents hadn't ordered her back when she'd called home to say where we were and why. She was smart, she was tough, but in many ways she was just a kid. I should've taken that into account before I hired her. But in the eyes of the state of California, Chelle was an adult, capable of making her own decisions. And she so badly wanted to buy that house she was planning to rehab. A steady job was the only way, and God knows I had plenty of work for her.

I went to the door of the dark house I was seeking, pressed the bell. No sound within—probably the ringer wasn't working. I knocked, waited. Footsteps sounded, soft and tentative. A young female voice asked, "Who's there?"

"Sharon McCone. I need to talk with Mr. J. T. Verke."

"He's not home."

"Can you tell me when he'll be back?"

"I don't...know." The voice seemed to be wavering on the edge of tears.

"Are you Mrs. Selena Verke?"

A harsh laugh, older than the years her voice projected. "As if I would wanta be."

"Who are you?" I asked.

"Who are *you*?"

"Sharon McCone, a private investigator who needs to contact Mr. Verke. Are you okay?"

"No."

"Can I help?"

"I don't know."

"Let me try."

"Do you have any ID?"

"Yes. I can slide it under the door to you."

"Okay."

I did, and after a long silence the porch light flicked on. I could sense her staring at me through the peephole. Finally a safety chain rattled and the door opened. A dark-haired girl of no more than thirteen looked out at me. She had a black eye turning yellow-green around the edges, several other facial bruises, and a chipped front tooth.

"I'm Gwen Verke," she said. "J. T.'s my father."

"May I come in?"

She hesitated.

"It's cold out here."

"Okay, I guess."

In the light she turned on in the entryway, the girl looked even more badly injured; she held her right arm at a stiff angle and winced as she handed my ID back to me with her left, then cradled her elbow.

"Did your father do this to you?" I motioned at her face.

"No."

"Who did?"

"My mother and her boyfriend."

"Are they here?"

"Not anymore."

"What does that mean?"

Her gaze wavered from mine, then dropped, and she began to cry. Not ordinary tears, but great heaving sobs between frantic gulps for air. I slipped through the door and shut it behind me. When I tried to touch her, she jerked away as if she were afraid of being burned. She backed up against the far wall, slid to the floor, rested her injured arm on her knees, her face in the opposite hand.

After a moment she got her crying under control and said, "I don't know whether I can trust you or not, lady, but I need help. Do I ever!"

"I'll see what I can do."

Gwen Verke led me to a door at the back of the house, opened it, and flicked on an overhead light. It revealed a cluttered one-car garage where tools, three lawn mowers, worn furniture, and packing boxes were jumbled together. Just like my family's garage in the old San Diego house used to be: no room for a car. It had always embarrassed me to have a family that couldn't get organized enough to dispose of the things that they didn't want or need anymore—the reason I used to delight in trips to Goodwill or the hospice thrift store.

Gwen stood next to me, silent. Staring down at a rolled and tied tarp near the overhead door. The top rope had been loosened and the canvas pulled back about six inches.

I said, "Is that what you want me to see?"

She nodded. I went over and took a look.

A woman's face confronted me, eyes open and blank, features stiffened into an expression of surprise.

Jesus! Melinda Knowles—Piper's supposed aunt.

I put my fingers to the cold neck, felt nothing but the hardness of rigor mortis nearing its peak.

I stood and went back to Gwen. "How did she get here?"

"I don't know. I came out here half an hour ago for some books that I had packed up. That…thing wasn't here this morning before I left for school, so I looked, and—" She started to cry again, but not as badly as before. This time when I put my hand on her shoulder she didn't pull away.

"Do you know who she is?"

"No."

"Did you call the police?"

"No. I was going to, but…I just couldn't."

"Okay. Why don't you go back inside? I'll check a couple of things and join you."

"I'm afraid to be in there alone. I'm afraid of everything nowadays."

Her battered face and chipped tooth gave her plenty of reason to be afraid. Yet she said she'd been to school. Why hadn't somebody there contacted Child Welfare?

"You say your mother and her boyfriend hurt you. When?"

"Last Thursday. They'd been here off and on, and he scared me. I had to lock my bedroom door. When I threatened to tell my dad, they beat me up and ran off. I don't think they're coming back; they've been talking about going to live in Mexico."

"And your dad?"

"I haven't seen much of him since the divorce. I used to have a phone number, but it's been out of service for six months now. What I said to Mom, it was just so that bastard would leave me alone."

"You tell anybody about your mom and her boyfriend beating you up? A teacher or counselor at school?"

She hung her head. "No. I didn't go until today, and when they asked, and I said I'd fallen on my face when I was skateboarding."

"And they believed that?"

"I think they wanted to. They don't want any trouble, and neither do I."

What the hell had happened to the people who were supposed to guard our children? Budget cuts and low staff morale were no excuse.

"Your dad—what does he do for a living?"

"He said he couldn't talk about it. And he wasn't here much even when he and Mom were married. I liked to think he was a spy, like James Bond."

"Does he own a van? An old Econoline?"

"No, that's Mom's. She and...that boyfriend went off in his SUV—it's brand-new. The van was in the driveway on Friday night, but it was gone on Saturday morning. I guess Mom came back for it."

Or someone else had.

Gwen Verke added, "But she didn't come back for me."

My God, was there no end to the cruelty parents inflicted on their children? I slipped my arm around the girl.

"What am I gonna do about this?" she asked, leaning into me. "I can't just leave that... thing there, but if I call the cops I'm afraid they'll think I killed her."

"Why would you kill a perfect stranger and hide her body in a tarp in the garage? How could you do that? You must weigh— what?—ninety pounds. You just tell them what you told me, and it'll be okay."

"Not so okay, maybe. Even if they don't think I killed that woman, they won't let me stay here alone. And I can't stay any- way because I don't have any money, except for ten bucks I bor- rowed off my best friend today. But they'll stick me in juvenile hall or foster care. I've got friends that had that happen to them. It's scary—"

"You just let me deal with the police. I can work something out."

Here you go, McCone—championing yet another bird with a bro- ken wing. Well, that's all right, you're broken in your own way.

"Now go inside," I added. "I'll be here the whole time. If you need me, all you have to do is call out."

I waited till the door closed behind her, then went over to the tarp. Snapped on one of the pairs of latex gloves that I keep in my bag and pulled the flaps back. The rigid, surprised expression on the woman's face and the cracked glasses secured by one earpiece made me look away toward the rest of her body, trying to see how she'd died.

Dried blood on her pink T-shirt. Knife or bullet, straight into the heart. Craig had found a bullet hole in the wall of the second- floor apartment at Piper's building. The unspoken consensus was that someone had shot Adah there. Now I felt a glimmer of hope. Perhaps the man in the apartment had shot Knowles, not Adah.

I covered her and looked around the garage for a weapon. None visible. I stepped over a cardboard carton and scrutinized the shelves that lined the far wall. Paint cans with hardened drips, a lamp with its socket and bulb hanging, various mostly rusty tools, garden supplies. I didn't want to compromise the scene any more than I already had, so I took out my phone and called 911.

Shortly before the first squad car arrived, I called Chelle and alerted her to what had happened. "Do you think you could come down here and comfort a thirteen-year-old?"

"Sure. Be right there."

Chelle was going to be a big asset until my driver's license was reinstated. Maybe until she got her real-estate empire going.

My cell rang. Hy.

"Where the hell are you? Why haven't you checked in? It's bad enough with Adah missing—"

"I'm following up on a lead. Any news about Adah or Piper?"

"I'd've called if there was. But you, it's late, and I've heard nothing. Didn't you think I'd be worried about you?"

"Of course, if I'd had time to think. But, Ripinsky, I'm onto something—"

"Something more important than me being reassured of your safety?"

He was right, but this scenario was getting old, I was tired, and I had a lot to contend with.

"I'm not a little kid who needs to check in with her daddy, Ripinsky." The words came spilling out, ungoverned.

Silence. I knew he was gritting his teeth, taking time to formulate a reply. Hy never impulsively lashed out like I did.

"Okay," he said at length. "Where's the MG? You're not driving it, are you?"

"No, I'm not driving. The MG is with Ted. I borrowed his Smart car. And Chelle is driving it."

"Chelle?"

A plainclothesman was looking impatiently at me.

"Yes, I hired her as my driver. I'll explain later. Right now I'm in the middle of something."

"What? Where?—"

"I'll call you."

The detective approached me. In that instant I decided I would tell him I'd come to interview Verke because he was a witness to a minor property-damage case. No more than that.

HY RIPINSKY

He paced around the kitchen, trying to calm himself. Then he smashed his fist into the stovetop, winced, and cradled it against the pain. When his hand had stopped throbbing, he called next door to Michelle Curley's house. Yes, her mother told him, Chelle had phoned and said Shar had hired her as a driver. They were in the South Bay, Cupertino.

Great. An eighteen-year-old had the sense to let her family know her whereabouts, but not his wife.

Shar had said she'd borrowed Ted's car and the MG was with him. Well, he could understand why: the restored classic was too noticeable and over the past year had had spates of unreliability. Maybe she'd told Ted exactly where she was going and why.

He tried Ted's number, but the line was busy. Still busy five minutes later.

The hell with it. He grabbed his jacket and headed out. Inaction wasn't his strong suit—never had been.

Plum Alley was one of San Francisco's hidden treasures. A short block perched high on Tel Hill, with splendid Art Deco buildings on one side, and a sheer drop-off on the other. Sweeping bay views and very little parking.

He was driving a new Range Rover, purchased just the month

before when his Mustang had crapped out. It was a great all-purpose vehicle, but no way was it going to fit into any of the slim spots on the alley. He had to park three blocks away from Ted's building, and even then it was a squeeze.

Still, it felt good to get out and walk in the cold, suddenly foggy air. It would clear his head. Cool his anger too.

Why? he thought. *Why, why, why?*

The word took on a cadence with the pounding of his feet on the sidewalk.

Why wouldn't Shar let him in? Let him help her?

What had happened to their closeness? And her closeness to the others who cared about her?

Trying to prove something. To herself, to him, to the rest of them. To the world.

Trying to prove she was the woman she used to be.

Wouldn't he, under the circumstances, do the same? Suppose he'd been in the wrong place at the wrong time, as Shar had. Been shot and spent months in a locked-in state, where he could hear, feel, and think, but never respond. Made his way back in spite of the serious medical and emotional handicaps. And then found that even those closest to him had lost faith in his abilities.

He wouldn't do well at all. He'd rail at the injustice of it; wallow in self-pity; then buck up and go crashing forward as if nothing had changed. But it would have—forever, in certain ways—and eventually he'd have to accept that.

Crashing forward was the stage Shar was at, he thought. But it was verging on acceptance: Hiring Chelle to drive her. Investigating within her abilities. Asking Adah's help when she came up against something she couldn't handle.

So why couldn't she rely on him?

He thought of her words on the phone: *I'm not a little kid who needs to check in with her daddy, Ripinsky.*

They echoed in his mind, unpleasantly clear. He *had* been acting more of a father to her than a husband, best friend, and lover.

The others had taken on the roles of doting aunts and uncles. And she—the indulged child—had finally rebelled.

He entered the courtyard of Ted's building, rang for the creaky gilded elevator in its glass block enclosure, and waited. Maybe Ted could help him make sense of the situation.

"I think I know what she's up to," Ted said. "I did a little detecting tonight."

They were seated in big thirties-style armchairs in his living room, each holding what Ted called a "therapeutic beer."

God, Hy thought, he must've looked like a maniac when Ted opened the door. His first reaction after he admitted him was to go to the kitchen and return with the bottles.

"So what did you detect?" he asked.

He knew that in recent years Ted had flirted with becoming an investigator. But he also knew Ted would never consider abandoning his post as Grand Poobah of the agency to become an operative. McCone Investigations was his kingdom, which he ruled benevolently.

Ted said, "I made a list of possibilities and then I accessed the files on the case, as well as Shar's e-mail. There's a file from Derek on it. Preliminary backgrounding on a J. T. Verke and, later, all the Verkes in the area."

"Who?"

"I don't know where she got the name, but it must have something to do with Adah's disappearance. Piper's too."

"Does this J. T. Verke live in Cupertino?"

"That's what the property search said."

Hy shook his head. Shar was back on the job big-time. He wasn't sure how he felt about that, but he wouldn't try to stop her. Not anymore.

"You want to see the report?" Ted asked.

Hy hesitated. He'd never understood the agency's policy of open access to other people's files. They all cooperated on certain cases, but there was bound to be sensitive information that shouldn't be shared. Of course, his skepticism said a lot about his own organization: high-level international security firms depended on the trust of their clients; absolute discretion was a necessity. No one at RI but Hy—not the managers of the branch offices around the world, not even his most loyal assistants—could tap into everything that was contained in their database. The words "on a need-to-know basis" were gospel.

"No. McCone's on top of this one. Anything from Craig?"

"Nothing since this morning—not surprising. He's a solitary investigator, likely to hold back information, particularly now, when it concerns Adah's safety."

Safety? What was safety? Hy didn't know anymore. And maybe he never had.

All those years making runs that would've burned out the typical charter pilot. The massacre at the jungle airstrip. The short time he was married to Julie, never feeling secure because he knew she was going to die of multiple sclerosis. His out-of-control behavior at the environmental protests after she passed, the jail time. And then there was McCone....

They'd endured dangerous and scary times, but they'd also had periods of peace. Long, lazy days at Touchstone. Soaring through perfect skies. Riding across the meadow at the ranch. Loving each other.

And then a bullet to her brain had changed it all....

Ted interrupted his painful train of thought. "Mick's under the radar too, but I think he had a date."

"A date?"

"Don't look so censorious. You were young and horny once too."

Hy smiled at the memories Ted's statement called up. "Yeah, and now I'm middle-aged and horny."

Ted gave him an enigmatic smile. "Back to the investigation. I want you to look at the list I made earlier...."

MICK SAVAGE

Alison's condo was not one of the priciest in the Millennium Tower—those were on the higher floors, culminating in penthouses that cost upward of twelve million—but it was spacious and well laid out, and the views were spectacular. The dinner had been catered by the five-star Michael Mina restaurant—RN74—on the ground floor.

"I got lucky," Alison told him as they sat sipping wine and watching the city lights through a swirling fog. "The units here went on sale at the depth of the recession, and they were offering a fifteen percent discount. My grandma had died and left me enough for a down payment—so here I am."

He'd been comparing this to his own condo: hers was urban chic, his old and shabby. Alison's place had natural beechwood floors, towering high ceilings, huge glass walls, limestone windowsills, granite counters, and Wolf appliances in the kitchen. But now he took a closer look around and noticed the sparse furnishings and lack of pictures on the walls. And when he'd arrived the absence of cooking smells made everything seem sterile.

Alison interpreted his glance. "Yeah, I can't afford to buy good furniture, so I'm doing it one piece at a time. I don't know, Mick, when I first saw the condo I fell in love with it. But now I'm wondering if I didn't fall in love with a lifestyle. And I'm not sure it suits me."

"Why not?"

"I'm a country girl from Indiana, as I've told you. Came here and bought into the big-city dream. So now I've got more space than I can fill, a twenty-four-seven concierge ready to book reservations or buy theater tickets I don't want, a health club I don't have the time to use, and the people…I don't have anything in common with them. It's not the right fit for me, but I don't know what is."

Her brow was creased, her mouth turned down. She looked so genuine and earnest that it warmed him. He moved closer—

And his phone rang.

He'd already told Alison that he would have to take any calls that came in tonight, since there was a crisis at the agency. He grimaced and answered it. Hy.

"I know you're on a date, but we can really use your help."

"I told Ted I'd be available."

"Derek did a preliminary backgrounding for Shar on a J. T. Verke, last-known address Valle Vista Street in Cupertino. I can't reach him—Derek, I mean—so…"

"Okay, all you have is the initials?"

"Correct."

"It's not a common last name, but still…Let me run it. Any profession you want me to index it to?"

"Security, all types."

"I'll get back to you soon." He turned to Alison. "Something I've got to do." He'd told her no details of the case, but stressed that it was urgent.

"I understand."

Did she? Most women wouldn't, not on the first real date.

"Really, I do." She squeezed his arm. "Call me when you get the chance."

"The dinner was wonderful. Next time it's at my place. Nothing fancy, but I'm a pretty good cook…." Jesus, he was babbling!

"Mick, go do what you have to."

A dismissal, or an invitation to resume at a future time? Damn, he wished he could read women like he could a computer.

Even with the new software it was taking a long time to get anything on J. T. Verke.

He leaned back in his chair, contemplating the situation. Behind him the TV muttered. He'd turned it on when he came back to his condo. He did that a lot now that he lived alone, mainly for background noise. Symptom of the lonely man he was becoming— would become, if Alison blew him off. He didn't think he had the heart to make many more forays into the urban singles scene.

The program was still running. He glanced over his shoulder at the TV.

National news—dull. Thank God. On that front, less was more.

He checked the search, listened to the state news. Same as usual—screwups and more screwups. Local news—

He swiveled around and stared at the TV screen.

A bagged body was being removed from a crappy-looking house in the South Bay. Cupertino.

Female victim, unidentified. Shot point-blank in the heart. Discovered in the attached garage by the homeowner's daughter. Homeowner's name being withheld until he could be contacted.

And there *she* was in the background.

He groaned.

His aunt. She'd goddamn done it again!

ADAH JOSLYN

She scrabbled back into a corner just before the door opened and she saw the same dark bulky shape that had leaned into the storage space silhouetted against a very dim light behind him. The bulb that she'd left on in the bathroom didn't reach far enough to illuminate his features. He didn't speak, just set something on the floor and backed out. She smelled food—beef and onions. Potatoes.

Adah remained still, listening. The only sound was the dripping and an occasional creak.

After a moment her hunger got the better of her and she crawled over to whatever the man had left her. A tray, containing a burger, fries, and a bottle of water. She warned herself to go slow; it was heavy food and wouldn't stay down if she wolfed it. When she'd finished, she felt queasy anyway.

She groped along the clammy wall and into the bathroom, sure she'd throw up. The food stayed down, however uncomfortably. After a while she felt better and once again began to search for something she might use as a weapon when her captor returned.

One of the bolts that held the toilet in place might be effective, but she'd examined them before, found them rusted in place. Now she set about loosening them, but only succeeded in breaking her last remaining long fingernail.

Well, shit.

She listened, heard the dripping sound again. It didn't come from any of the fixtures. What was this place anyway? It reminded her of a sleeping compartment on a train, although marginally larger. The facilities were old, maybe of 1980s vintage or earlier; the floors in the bathroom were a linoleum popular back then. The paneling in the other room was cheap veneered stuff, and some of it had been pulled away, exposing seamed and riveted metal.

Her clothes reeked and her armpits smelled of sweat. Again she considered using the shower, then discarded the idea. Her reflexes were poor and her mind wasn't working too well. If her captor surprised her, she wouldn't be able to focus on defending herself. The aftereffect of the drugs, she supposed.

Earlier she'd thought she was only minutes from being killed, but now she'd been fed. Apparently her captor was going to let her live a while longer.

Why? What good was she to him? Why, for that matter, had she been allowed to live at all?

No-brainer.

He'd seen her ID. He knew who she was. Operative with McCone Investigations, former SFPD homicide investigator. She'd been a big deal while with the department because she was a woman and black—half Jewish too—and they'd trotted her out for a lot of photo ops. Whoever this guy was must assume that if he killed her and her body was found, they'd hunt him down ruthlessly.

Little did he know.

Well, that was a bargaining point if she ever got to talk with the man. Or the woman—Eva—who'd injected her in the first place. But all her instincts told her the guy was alone, had been for some time now.

Of course, there might be another reason he wanted her alive: he thought she had information about Piper's disappearance or Piper herself. But then why hadn't he interrogated her? Was he saving her for someone else, perhaps a person who'd hired him?

She resumed her search, this time for something stronger than her fingernails to pry the toilet bolts loose. But she quickly became disoriented and off balance, her vision blurred.

Bastard had probably put something in the bottled water.

She was barely able to crawl to the makeshift bed before she passed out.

MICK SAVAGE

He was making progress on the J. T. Verke search when somebody pounded on the condo's door. He went over there in bare feet, looked through the peephole. Craig.

When he opened the door Craig rushed through. "I've got a sketch of the perp," he said, "and I've scanned it and sent it out to the appropriate people. But I need you to see if you can identify him."

Mick motioned to his monitor. "I'm in the middle of a search. Can't interrupt it."

"Derek, then. Get Derek to help out."

The man sounded desperate. He hadn't shaved or changed his clothes or combed his hair since the morning Adah disappeared. Mick said, "You look like you could use some food or a drink."

Craig waved the suggestion away. "What I need is somebody to help me identify this sketch."

Mick studied it. The man looked vaguely familiar. "Where'd you get this?"

He listened as Craig explained. "McCone's onto something too," he added. "She was canvassing the same area."

"You bet she's onto something." He related what he'd seen on the news. "I haven't been able to reach her, but I suspect this murder has to do with J. T. Verke, the guy I'm running the search on."

"So can you get hold of Derek—?"

"No. He called half an hour ago; his grandmother died tonight and he's on a flight to LA."

"Great timing."

"Well, I suppose it was inconvenient for her too."

"Sorry." Craig sat down on the futon, head in hands. "I'm just so afraid for Adah."

"I know." Behind Mick his monitor beeped, signaling incoming information. "Okay, now I can interrupt the search for Verke and get started on your man." He went to the screen, looked at what was displayed there.

"Well, what d'you know," he said. "Verke's former CIA. And he's not your guy. There's a photo. Big, mostly bald, and mean looking."

Craig was peering over his shoulder. "What division of the agency?"

"Special Activities. I don't know anything about them."

"I do." And all of it was alarming. "SAD is an umbrella department. You can find out about them on official government Web sites. There're nice detailed explanations about what they do, but they don't tell you who else is under the umbrella—deep, covert agencies that'll never be mentioned, even in top CIA circles."

"Like what?"

"If I knew, the rest of the world would. One example: you've heard about the assassination program that they kept secret for years? That wasn't anything new. They've had a license to kill since the fifties."

"You're kidding. What else?"

"Run a search on my man for CIA connections, and then I'll tell you more."

WEDNESDAY, FEBRUARY 11

SHARON McCONE

Gwen Verke cried out in her sleep—a wrenching sound that echoed the way I felt. I looked at Hy, then went along the hallway to the guest room at the front of the house. She'd settled down, so I left the door open a crack and returned to the sitting room.

It was nearly one in the morning. After lengthy questioning, the Cupertino Police and Child Protective Services had temporarily released Gwen into my custody. She'd protested any other arrangement so strongly, and I'd supported her, so they'd bent the rules. Besides, one of them had whispered to me, since I'd earned the girl's trust, maybe I could find out details about the mother and father. I doubted she knew much more than she'd told me, but I said I'd try.

Gwen had been so tired that she fell asleep in the squad car that delivered us to my house, leaving Chelle to drive back alone. With relief I noted Ted's Smart car in the driveway next door. Hy was home and he'd seen the evening news; he said nothing about my lack of communication, and helped me settle Gwen in. Since then we'd been talking about the investigation and waiting for calls to come in from various contacts.

I sat down beside Hy again, sighing deeply. On the hearth the embers of the fire were glowing deep red.

"She'll be okay," Hy said. "Anybody who can talk down social workers the way you said she did can weather a few nightmares."

"Hope so." I recalled some of my own nightmares, then banished that line of thought. "Mick's confirmed that J. T. Verke is formerly CIA. My theory is that J. T.'s been gone from the Bay Area since the divorce, but came back on assignment and took that van from his ex-wife's driveway late Friday night or early Saturday. Reasonable that he would still have a key."

"But is it reasonable that he'd use a vehicle that could be traced back to him?"

"Everybody makes mistakes. He probably assumed the ex had reregistered it in her name."

"His first mistake. Second was leaving evidence at the scene of Adah's abduction. But his worst mistake was leaving the Knowles woman's body in his ex-wife's garage. Why the hell would he do such a thing?"

"Maybe he planned to move it. Or didn't put it there in the first place."

"Who did, then?"

"Somebody who wanted to implicate him? I don't know."

Hy looked at his watch. "God, I wish Trent would call back."

Sometimes you get what you ask for. His phone rang.

"Trent. What've you got?"

I watched his face; it was impassive throughout the conversation except for a small tic of surprise. No wonder he was such a good hostage negotiator. Even here, in his own home with me, he didn't give much away.

When he ended the call he said, "A low-level local executive protection agency—Morell Associates—handled the cleanup at Piper's building. They're efficient but not top echelon."

"Why would the CIA—or whoever—use a firm like that?"

"Puts distance between them and the abductions. It's not an uncommon practice. You remember the Blackwater mess. They hired a North Carolina firm for seven years to conduct antiterrorist operations overseas—and ended up netting zero terrorists."

Hy's phone rang again. "Yeah, Trent...Jesus."

He listened quietly again, broke the connection.

"Well, that proves we're up against something big. Morell's three top people were en route to a conference in Denver tonight when their plane crashed in the Rockies. There's nobody with any authority left at their headquarters here in the city."

"My God! So if they work on a need-to-know basis, the crash took out the only people who could possibly tell us what happened to Adah or Piper."

He nodded. "Which leads me to suspect that the crash was no accident. It resembles other ploys the CIA has used to get rid of witnesses—or gain control over a situation that's gotten out of hand."

"So who has the two of them? CIA or some low-level Morell operatives?"

"Hard to say. The CIA probably has Piper; for whatever reason, she was their primary target. They may have Adah too. If by chance the security personnel have either one, it's a bad situation. The operatives are out there with no one to report to. And those people, I'll tell you, are not the best and the brightest."

"So they'll be desperate." I closed my eyes and felt hot tears dribble down my cheeks. Damn! Even now, eight months after I'd been shot, my emotions ran out of control at times of stress. Would it ever stop?

I said, "If they haven't killed them already, now they're sure to."

"McCone, don't think that way. I don't know about Piper, but Adah's strong and streetwise. If she's alive, she'll talk or muscle her way out of this—just as that kid sleeping in the guest room did with the social workers."

"Social workers are one thing. These people are capable of doing anything to ensure their survival."

Hy was silent. He'd lived in the shadowy world of high-level security too long not to know to what extremes some operatives would go.

After a moment he said, "We'd better get some sleep. Today's already starting out to be difficult."

"Sleep isn't an option. I'm calling a staff meeting and you're going to start surveillance on Morell."

He put his fingers under my chin, tipped my head, and looked into my eyes. "You're all the way back, aren't you?"

"Ripinsky, it feels as if I've never been away."

CRAIG MORLAND

His hands were shaking from too much coffee, and his eyes burned. Mick had been hunched over his keyboard for almost fifteen minutes while Craig paced.

The phone rang and Mick said, "Get that, will you?"

Ted. "Staff meeting in an hour, Mick. Bring everything you've got."

"It's Craig. Mick and I may be onto something; we'll be there."

When he relayed the information, Mick asked, "Who called the meeting?"

"Shar, I guess."

"So she's with us again. I suspected as much."

"With us with a vengeance. Too bad it took a goddamn tragedy to bring her back."

Mick winced visibly at the bitterness in Craig's voice. He said, "It's not a tragedy yet. Don't get into that mode."

"You having any luck identifying the sketch?"

"None. But I know I've seen this guy somewhere." A pause. "Christ, look at this site!"

Craig peered over his shoulder. Photograph of a man in jeans, a flak vest, and a knitted cap crouching and aiming what looked to be an M4. Captioned "William 'Jesse' James, SAD operative in Afghanistan." Various comments were posted on the site.

You kick ass, Jesse!

Awesome outfit and firepower!

I wanted a semi-automatic for a while because I stabbed a guy to death last week and now I want to shoot one.

Hey, sweet William, how about a little?

Makes me want to blow somebody away too.

I love hunky guys who kill.

The comments were equally divided between men and women.

"What kind of crap is this?"

"Fan site for CIA paramilitary," Mick said. "These guys in the photos aren't really with the agency; it's all staged. But it shows the fascination people have for them."

"I didn't realize they had a fan club. Seriously sick."

"So tell me more about the Special Activities Division."

"Like I said, it's an umbrella agency. Their official mission is to conduct paramilitary operations and political influence campaigns in worldwide hot spots. Their paramilitary operatives are out there without a net, no uniforms, nothing to connect them to our government—which in most cases disavows them if they're caught."

"But this Verke is a former SAD operative and working within the country. Doesn't wash."

"The CIA has not been known to respect boundaries."

"Yeah. So this group—SAD—is open about their mission."

"No. They also conduct very covert operations under various guises."

"Such as?"

"For one, in the sixties, the Health Alteration Committee—its mission was to kill the then-leader of Iraq. They sent him a poisoned handkerchief. Didn't work, and I pity the underling in the mail room who absconded with it. For years, their executive action unit tried to kill Fidel Castro—inane plots such as exploding cigars and a contaminated diving suit. For eight years they concealed from Congress their vice-presidentially approved plans to take out the leaders of Al-Qaeda. And their 1997 manual on killing makes interesting reading."

Mick shook his head.

"Fortunately, the agency isn't very good with elaborate plots and high-level killing. None of their major efforts has succeeded." Craig's head had begun to ache. "Let's get over to the pier for the meeting."

HY RIPINSKY

Morell Associates' offices were located in a warehouse on Palou Avenue, a block off Third Street in the largely industrial Bayshore district. He'd gotten the address and promotional information on the firm from their Web site. To one unfamiliar with executive protection, it would've looked great: their list of clients and services was impressive and Morell's bio boasted of twenty years' experience with the NSA.

And it was mostly bullshit. Morell Associates' best-known clients were rock stars for whom they'd provided guards when the groups were performing in the Bay Area. They were less an executive protective firm than a security outfit. Two badly bungled jobs had laid them open for lawsuits that they'd settled out of court. And Kurt Morell's stint with the NSA had been as a low-level attorney and of only five years' duration. Add what Hy had already known about them to the location of their offices, and it spelled losers. With a capital L.

He hadn't had much reason to visit the area, but he'd familiarized himself with a map. The Bayshore, he knew, was predominately black and subject to all the ills of a community of poor, under- or unemployed minorities. Young men with no viable futures turned to drugs and gang violence; young women had their men's babies and grieved when their husbands or lovers died or went to prison; mothers were strong, but there was little they could do to keep their boys off the streets; fathers were largely absent.

A waste, Hy called it, a fucking waste. It didn't have to be that way, but few people cared about these poverty-ridden, crime-plagued pockets of the city. Those who did didn't have the where-withal or influence to do anything about them.

The majority of the warehouse was dark—Morell apparently shared the space with a trucking firm—but the section at the rear was brightly lighted. He avoided a pothole in the street, pulled to the curb, and started back there on foot. Crouching behind a Dumpster, he peered through the windows.

A short-haired blonde woman sat at the reception desk, face buried in her hands. The phone rang, and she picked up, spoke briefly. From his vantage Hy saw that she was in her twenties, her face blotchy from crying; she took a tissue from a box on the desk and blew her nose. Grieving for her employers? In any case, why was she here at this hour?

Hy had called a buddy at the FAA before he left the house, but he couldn't tell him much, just that the weather had been clear when the small jet went down. Pieces of the plane and bodies were scattered all over a mountainside and the NTSB's investigation would take weeks, even months, to complete.

Mountain flying was dangerous under the best of conditions. Downdrafts, updrafts, unexpected snowstorms or high winds aloft. McCone, a better pilot than he, remained wary of it because of a near crash in the Tehachapis years before. Hy didn't mind it because after he'd met Shar he'd come to believe that he wasn't going to die anywhere but in bed as a very old man. That, among other things, was what love was about—the determination to make it in the long run.

But accidents still happened to other people....

The cause of the crash could have been simple pilot error or something more sinister. The NTSB might never find out the exact circumstances because, unlike the big passenger planes, jets of that size weren't equipped with black boxes, and the pilot hadn't contacted Denver Control. The only certainty was that three passengers and the pilot were dead.

Hy went up to the door, knocked, and entered. The blonde woman looked up in surprise.

"Don't you know it's not a good idea to leave the door unlocked when you're here alone at night?" he asked.

She stared.

"Hy Ripinsky, Ripinsky International." He placed his card on the desk. "I heard about the plane crash, saw the lights, and thought, as a colleague in the industry, that I might be of assistance."

"Irene Aguirre. I'm the office manager."

"Why are you here at"—he consulted his watch—"one-thirty in the morning?"

"I got a call about the crash; the man asked that I come in to field phone inquiries. He told me he'd be in touch with details. So far, nobody's called except the *Chronicle*, and I had nothing to tell them."

"The man didn't identify himself?"

"No. His voice sounded vaguely familiar. But no."

"Is there anything I can do?"

"Find out something I can tell people."

Briefly he outlined what his buddy at the FAA had told him. By the time he was done, tears were leaking from her eyes again.

"Tell me, Ms. Aguirre, was the agency working on something unusual or highly secret recently?"

"I don't know. Maybe. Mr. Morell sent me out for an early lunch a few times, and when I got back I noticed that he'd had a conference in his office. Extra coffee cups, you know."

"Did you ask him about them?"

"Oh, no! The rule here is don't ask."

"Need-to-know basis?"

She smiled weakly. "That pretty much describes it."

"So what are you going to do now?"

"Stay here, in case the man calls again. I couldn't sleep, anyway."

"Okay, call me if you hear from your mystery man, and I'll let you know if I find out anything more."

He waited in a dark corner of the parking lot. It was only twenty minutes before a white car pulled in and parked in a similarly dark place. A tall, thick-bodied, blond-haired man in jeans and a fringed jacket got out and went into the office. Hy crept forward.

The man was standing over Irene Aguirre, gesturing widely. She looked up at him, shaking her head. Hy moved closer. The window was open a crack, and he could hear parts of their conversation.

Aguirre: "...don't know."

"Got to be something in the files."

"There aren't any files. At least not any I can access on the computer. And if there were any paper files, Mr. Morell would have had them with him."

"Well, great, just great."

"I'm sorry."

"They left me out there without a safety net. What the fuck am I supposed to do now? No contact information? No nothing?"

"He never gave me anything." She paused. "You're the one who called me and told me to come into the office, right?"

"I don't know what you're talking about."

"You are. I recognize your voice."

"You don't recognize nothin', bitch!"

Hy ran back to his Rover and waited. The big man came out of the office and strode to his car.

It wasn't until Hy had started tailing him that he realized the car was a white Prius, license number 5111234.

Adah's car.

SHARON McCONE

Thirty-six hours," I said to my assembled staff. "I know the odds are that Adah's dead. Piper too. If they were being held by some low-level security person with Morell Associates and they haven't already been killed, he or she is out there without direction or authority, scared as hell, and wants them off their hands."

As I spoke I could feel the chill that had come over the room. I glanced around the table, making eye contact with each of them. Craig looked determined but haggard; I was certain he hadn't slept in two days. Patrick had hung up yet another flow chart, and his hands shook as he added a few notations. Mick held some notes, jotted down a few words. Ted sat up straight, eyes fixed on the wall behind me. Thelia was alert and ready to tackle the problem at hand.

"But those are only odds," I went on. "All of you know Adah's strength and determination. She's survived a situation like this before, and I'm betting that she'll survive the current one."

Each nodded at me, believing. God, maybe I had a future as an inspirational speaker! But I had faith in what I'd said. I *had* to believe it to keep functioning.

"We're here to pool our information. Also theories and wild-hair ideas. Remember: anything, no matter how small, can lead to a solution. Mick?"

"J. T. Verke, the man whose van was sighted leaving Piper

Quinn's building late Sunday night, has been identified as a for-mer operative of the CIA's Special Activities Division. Craig can tell you more about them."

Craig explained that within SAD, there were two groups: one to exert covert political influence in sensitive areas of the world and the Special Operations Group, which conducted paramilitary operations. J. T. Verke had been classified as a Paramilitary Oper-ations Officer, indicating that he was with SOG.

So why was he running an operation within the United States?

"Special assignment?" I asked.

"Feels right to me. He could be attached to any unit under that umbrella."

"I think we can assume that Adah's disappearance is a product of her being in the wrong place at the wrong time. But Piper—why would the CIA be interested in her?"

"The husband," Mick said.

"The husband's dead."

"He was in intelligence. Maybe he told her something sensitive."

"Possibly. Any other ideas?"

Blank faces. Maybe conducting these meetings in the early hours of the morning was a mistake.

I said, "This was a fairly large operation, making not only a person but the residents of an entire apartment building disap-pear. What could be that important? What 'matter of national security'?"

Craig asked, "Another question—who's this man I have a sketch of? The one who was asking people in the neighborhood about Piper?"

"What about Morell Associates?" Mick added. "There must be some way we can connect them to Verke."

Patrick added a few notations and arrows to his flow chart.

Thelia said, "Paper trails. They always leave paper trails."

Ted said, "I made a list—"

Everybody ignored him and started talking at once.

"The husband. Got to find out more about him."

"J. T. Verke—where's he currently living?"

"The Knowles woman—must be CIA or former CIA too. Can we get the autopsy report and whatever information they may use to identify her?"

"Morell—got to find out more about them."

"How the hell can we go up against the CIA?"

"How? Because we're smarter."

"Well, that's a given—"

My phone rang. Hy.

"I just tailed a man from Morell Associates's offices," he said. "I think he may be the operative who has Adah."

"Tailed him to where?"

"A very secluded cottage—more like a shack—above Inverness, on the Point Reyes Seashore."

"Any indication she's being held there?"

"None. It's a small place, maybe three rooms, and there're lights on in all of them. There's a shed, but it looks like a strong wind would blow it over."

"You carrying?"

"You know I never do during routine operations."

"Well, it's not routine now. Are you in danger?"

"No. A woman drove up a few minutes ago, and they're drinking in what looks like the living room. I'm well covered, taking photos and running a surveillance."

"Photos on your BlackBerry?"

"Right."

"Send them to Mick."

"Will do."

"Give me directions, and I'll be there as quickly as I can."

As I said it, I thought, *But how?* This was a potentially dangerous situation. I couldn't bring Chelle into it; it was bad enough that I'd involved her in the aftermath of Melinda Knowles's murder last night.

I looked around the table. "Hy needs backup. Not you, Craig. You need to be here for Adah and to take calls from your contacts. Who will volunteer to drive me to Inverness?"

"I'll help," Mick said.

"No, I need you here doing searches. You too, Thelia."

Ted said, "Let me go."

"Okay, you're it."

He smiled, looking inordinately pleased.

I could guess what he was thinking: *The armchair detective rides again.*

ADAH JOSLYN

She'd very nearly gotten a bolt loose from the base of the toilet. Attribute that to the strength she'd gained from last night's meal. There must be a Mickey D's nearby—but then there was one everywhere. No clue as to where she was being held.

Her captor wouldn't be back till this evening, she was sure of that. He would come and go only in darkness to avoid being seen. Plenty of time to work on this bolt with the underwire she'd ripped from her bra.

Funny that she hadn't thought about the wire—either as a device to use in getting free or as a weapon—until she'd awakened to the bra's pinching and chafing under her breasts. She'd reached back to unhook the damned thing, and that was when she realized that underwire was extremely strong and resilient. And then in her jacket pocket, she'd found a tube of lip balm. He'd taken everything else, but either missed it or considered it too innocuous to bother with.

When you thought about it, women had certain strategic advantages over men. A man thought of a bra as only something he wanted to take off a woman, not as something a woman could take off and use to defend herself. A man thought of lip balm as something sticky that smeared when he kissed a woman, not as a lubricant with nearly the strength of WD-40.

Several applications of lip balm to the bolt had loosened the corrosion. She cleaned it out with the tip of the underwire and applied more, deep under the bolt where it would work on the rest of the rust. A lot of patience and a few more applications, and she might be able to twist the bolt off with her fingers.

She rested back on her heels and waited, staring at the bolt as if she could will it to move on its own.

TED SMALLEY

Inverness: a wide place on the road that followed the shore of Tomales Bay in west Marin County. Dark and foggy in the early hours of a winter morning. Wind-warped trees and shrubbery, houses on the shore and hills without light, faded yellow double line wavering along a snakelike country road. His sense of direction was lost in the mist, his sense of reality too. They could have been in another universe—one whose population had died out eons ago.

They: Shar and him. Two brave detectives off on a mission.

Who was he kidding? He was quaking in his cowboy boots and was afraid he might have to pull off the road and puke.

Part of it had been the drive: over the Golden Gate Bridge and up 101 to the Highway 1 turnoff. On a twisting, jarring ride along the high cliffs leading to Stinson Beach and Bolinas, a harrowing route that Ted, a confirmed urbanite, shuddered at even when someone else was at the wheel.

He tried to relax, make small talk.

"I've never been here. Have you?"

"A long time ago, on a case. You remember—when Hank's old friends were being killed off."

"Oh, yeah." He had good reason to remember that case; it was the first time he'd seen Shar act violently, and it had scared him, as well as the other folks at All Souls. Put a wall up between them and her—for a while."

"Then you realize things didn't end up well."

"The guy shot himself."

"Yes, and I've avoided this area ever since."

"But most of your cases don't turn out that way."

"Well, I've come out alive so far. And, as you know, very few of my clients have stiffed me on the fee. But sometimes what happens to the people involved is less than satisfying. To put it mildly."

"How so?"

"The case out here. And the one when I traced that Paso Robles woman who had been missing twenty-some years. What I found tore up her daughters' lives. The guy who was bombing RKI's offices—I couldn't stop him till he'd killed a lot of people. Involvement in a crime changes people, even if they're only connected peripherally. You find out what they're made of, and a lot of times it isn't good. You also find out what you're made of. The crime becomes a part of you that'll be with you the rest of your life."

"Why d'you do it, then?"

"It's what I do; it's who I am."

Ted slowed for the little town, although it was obvious he didn't need to. No cop was lurking in the fog to arrest speeders; the businesses were closed, most of the houses dark.

She said, "I'll start watching for the landmark Ripinsky gave me."

"Okay." All of a sudden he felt surprisingly calm. Shar was in control; he was safe. "What's my role in this? How can I help?"

"By staying in the car when we get there."

"But..."

"Stay in the car, Ted. Keep an eye out for any sign of trouble and if there is, head back to the pier."

"And just leave you here?"

"I'll be all right. Remember, I'll be with Ripinsky." A few minutes later she said, "Turn left by that mailbox shaped like a lighthouse."

The road wound steeply uphill through pines and bay laurels and oaks. Dark bulky shapes were all he could see of the houses. They appeared suddenly and then receded into the mist. Their ghostlike quality made him nervous all over again.

"Up there on the left," she whispered, "is a secondary road with about a dozen mailboxes at its foot. Hy should be waiting for us."

"Why are you whispering?"

"I don't know. Why am I? I guess because when it's this dark and deserted I feel like there are secret microphones everywhere."

"And I thought *I* was paranoid."

"Well, I guess it goes with the territory. Slow down—there're the mailboxes."

Mailboxes, but no Range Rover. No Hy either.

Anxiety nibbled at Ted, but he concealed it as Shar said, "We'll just pull over and wait."

Fifteen minutes and still no Hy. Shar said she didn't want to call his cell because he might have it on ring mode, and if he was still running his surveillance, it could give him away. But, Ted thought, Hy had run plenty of surveillances; surely he'd remembered to switch the phone to vibrate.

To cover his nervousness he chattered for a while about his new silk fashion statement. By the time he'd gotten to the problems of wrinkling and frequent dry cleaning, he knew she wasn't listening and felt silly. Maybe he was really just a trivial person. Maybe he didn't have empathy for others when they were in need.

Shar took his hand. "I'm glad you're the one who drove me."

He squeezed her hand. It was cold, so he took it into both of his and chafed some warmth into it.

After a while he said, "Wouldn't Hy have left his car down here and snuck up on them? That's a dead end road; he could get trapped."

"I've been thinking the same thing. Also Hy's unarmed; he has a carry permit but doesn't like to keep firearms on him unless he's anticipating serious trouble."

"But you're armed, right?"

"I brought my three-fifty-seven Magnum along tonight."

Her phone rang. "Mick," she said to him after a brief conversation. "The property at the address Hy gave me is owned by a Santa Barbara corporation. The whole tract on that road, in fact. Bayside Realty in Point Reyes Station manages the rentals. He's left a message on their voice mail—he'll call again as soon as he knows anything more."

"I heard you tell him to call my cell. Why?"

"Because I'm going up there."

Ted's pulse accelerated. "Maybe you should wait a little longer."

"No, I've waited long enough." She took her .357 from her bag.

Ted focused on the gun: ugly, gleaming in the red light from the GPS indicator on the dashboard. He'd seen her remove it dozens of times from the office safe, where Craig and Julia Rafael also kept their firearms. He knew she had a .38 in a lockbox at home. And Hy—God knew how many guns he possessed. None of them were nuts about weapons, but their ownership of them was enough to make him uncomfortable.

"Don't worry," she told him. "It's strictly a precaution."

He grabbed her arm. "Please don't go up there. Call the cops, the sheriff, whatever they have out here."

"You know I can't do that. Adah..."

Adah. Of course. In his anxiety he'd almost lost sight of her.

He clung to Shar's arm a moment longer, then said, "Go do what you have to. I'll be here waiting."

CRAIG MORLAND

He was losing his mind. He sincerely believed it.

In the next office, Mick was still working on identifying the sketch Roxanne Cramer had made. Still insisting the guy in it looked familiar. So why couldn't the kid remember where he'd seen him? He had a young, sharp mind, hadn't he?

In contrast, Craig's mind felt like mud. He'd been hunched over the computer, soaking up meaningless details about CIA covert operations, and alternatively taking calls from connections in DC. The notes he'd made during those calls were virtually indecipherable, the information jumbled.

Mud. Hardening by the hour.

When had he last slept? So long ago he couldn't recall. He'd tried to nap on the air mattress in the conference room; that had been no-go, and he was sure he couldn't sleep now. But sooner or later he'd crash. And then what good would he be to Adah, or anyone?

He was considering trying to nap again when his phone rang. A man he'd been referred to at the CIA, known to him only as Lyle.

"This J. T. Verke," Lyle said. "He was with SOG, but in the last year of the past administration was tapped for an operation called TRIAD—Terrorism Resistance and Investigative Assignment Division. A nasty bunch specializing in kidnappings, torture, murder—anything in the interests of keeping the right people in money and power. When Obama was elected, TRIAD was dis-banded, but apparently a number of their people went rogue, kept operating."

Craig's mind was no longer moving sluggishly. "Their objective?"

A laugh, rough and cynical. "What d'you think? Patriotism unbound. Preserve the status quo, no matter what it takes."

"You know anything else about them?"

"Hell, no. I've never heard of them. And you've never heard of me." The connection was broken.

Craig sat alert, tapping the desk with his fingertips. Mentally repeated acronyms: CIA, SAD, SOG. And now this new one: TRIAD.

Patriotism unbound.

And who were the right people who must be kept in money and power? Defense contractors, lobbyists, politicians with their hands out. Rich people who ran things from behind the scenes, who made large political contributions to ensure they stayed rich. And they were not all in this country either. Foreign interests had controlled much of American policy and probably still did, and the networks through which influence and cash were exchanged had grown more intricate, less detectable—unknown but to a select group of people, hidden from public and governmental scrutiny.

So what had Piper Quinn done to draw the attention of a rogue intelligence agency? Or more likely, what had her husband done?

ADAH JOSLYN

The bolt came loose and she pulled it out, clasped it in both hands like a talisman. Then she bent her head over it and cried a little.

So many hours, such reining in of her natural impatience. So much fear of the dead bolt turning and the underwire being snatched from her hands before she could hide it. So much fear of dying...

No time for crying now. She dried her face on her shirtsleeve, examined the bolt. Its end was flat, still corroded.

Some weapon.

She stared at it, hope fading. All that time, and what did she have but a rusty piece of junk? Useless, unless she could manage a lucky jab into her captor's eye. He—more likely they—would slap it out of her hand as if it were a toy gun.

Since when did you become such a defeatist? Your other kidnapper was a certifiable lunatic, but you practically talked him to death till help arrived.

That was different: these people are sane, professional, and even more deadly. They have weapons, drugs, and strength in numbers.

Or did they? There had been the woman, Eva, who attacked her on the stairs. The man in the upstairs apartment—his height and build weren't the same as the one who'd been tending to her. So maybe there was just this one man to contend with. If she had a weapon, a suitable weapon ... that and her self-defense skills could bring him down.

Adah looked at the bolt in her hand. There had to be something else she could use....

HY RIPINSKY

He never heard the man slip stealthily behind him. Didn't know he was there until the cold muzzle of a gun jabbed into his neck and a sharp voice commanded, "Make a move and I'll blow your head off."

Hy froze. There was nothing he could do but obey.

Shit! He'd been watching the woman who had arrived earlier leave the shack, and the man had gone out the back way and circled around behind him. Sleight-of-hand, the staple of any magician's repertoire. Stupid to have been taken in by it.

The man marched him across the uneven ground toward the house, searched him, and took his car keys, wallet, and BlackBerry. Pushed him into the ramshackle shed and shut the doors. Hy heard a padlock click shut, and then the man's voice said, "We'll have a little talk later, but there's something I gotta do first."

Darkness. Hy stared into it, waiting for his eyes to adjust. Tool shed—yard waste cans and a wheelbarrow, gas can and lawn mower, hammers and jars full of nails, clippers, and trimmers. And a shovel.

This guy isn't too bright.

He listened at the door. Footsteps crunching on the gravel of the long driveway. When they faded he hefted the shovel, felt its blade. Dull and rusted, but it would do.

He worked quickly, easing the shovel's blade into the small space between the double doors. The wood was termite-ridden and had plenty of give; the hasp didn't feel very secure in its moorings. Hy worked the blade back and forth until one side of the hasp pulled loose. Pushed through the doors, shovel extended in front of him. Didn't see anybody and started running.

Halfway to the line of pines, he heard the engine of his Range Rover coming up the hill and into the driveway. He raced for the woods, but he wasn't quick enough to avoid being seen in the moonlight. The Rover jerked to a stop and the man jumped out, shouting, and ran after him.

Hy glanced over his shoulder and saw the guy was armed with a short-barreled rifle. The shovel was slowing him down, so he jettisoned it; a shovel was no match for a high-powered weapon.

Through the trees, zigging and zagging, his breath searing in his lungs. Looking for a way out or a place to hide. But his pursuer knew the terrain better, was more sure-footed and gaining on him.

Ducking around the tree trunks, slapping at their branches. And still the gap was closing between them. A vine caught at his ankle but he didn't break stride, felt it trail out behind him until it broke. Seconds later he smacked into a tree trunk, and its rough surface cut his cheek. Blood slicked one side of his mouth as he ran.

Then suddenly he was in a clearing illuminated by murky dawn light. He scanned it swiftly, looking for cover. Ahead was a drop-off; to either side, more trees. The sounds of pursuit were close behind him.

Hy dodged to the right, but not before a bullet whined past his head and he heard the crack of the rifle. He tried to take evasive action too late. He felt a slamming pain in his shoulder an instant before the second report sounded.

The blow spun him around and he went down in a hard sprawl,

hurt but not totally disabled. He clawed one-handed at the ground, scrambled forward to the edge of what looked to be a ravine with steeply canted sides.

Get out of his line of fire. Tuck and roll downhill.

He tucked and rolled.

SHARON McCONE

The road was unpaved and rutted from recent rains, leading up into one of those enclaves that their residents term rustic because they have to slog through mud in their expensive vehicles to their multimillion-dollar homes. I'd always speculated their kind were like the nobles of Versailles playing peasants.

And an unpaved road kept the rabble out.

In spite of the rigorous climb, the lack of sleep, and my recent inactivity—I hadn't been to physical therapy since Adah disappeared—I felt strong and alert. Back all the way, Hy had said. Not quite, but almost. So I had to go slower and my breath turned ragged and occasionally I had to stop to rest—it was a far cry from lying inert and helpless.

Besides, Hy was somewhere up there on the hill. In trouble. I sensed it, in the way I'd always been able to.

No Range Rover parked up here either, and the road was narrowing, the dark shapes of the houses smaller. To the right side was a declivity, and I slid down into it, moving slowly through rocks and mud. Vegetation scratched at my face and hands, and a couple of times I almost fell to my knees. The road beside me kept climbing. I was breathing really hard now, sweating inside my microfiber jacket. The Magnum weighed heavily at my side. I stopped, shifted it from the pocket to inside the belt of my jeans, rested a bit, then went on.

Hy had described the house to which he'd followed the man he suspected of having taken Adah as the last one on the right, little better than a shack. Must be isolated, because I hadn't encountered a driveway in many yards. Now I came to a narrow wooden bridge—the bridge Hy had said led to the place. I touched one of its supports, and my hand stung from splinters. Above I saw missing boards, a sagging railing. I stopped and listened.

The sky had become lighter and birds were stirring in the trees above. A jay made a racket; he was awake and so should be the rest of the avian population. No human sounds yet, but I'd better make my move soon.

I scrambled up the side of the declivity and into a grove of pines, catching my foot on a protruding root and steadying myself on one of the trunks. My hand came away sticky and acrid with sap. The house—a small, boxy, one-story shape—was faintly visible through the trees. Lights on, but no activity.

I approached slowly, taking care not to snap twigs or crunch fallen cones. Stopped at the first row of trees.

Hy's Range Rover was parked near a shed to the side, and Adah's Prius stood beside it.

Wrong, very wrong.

I closed my eyes, replayed the conversation we'd had earlier. Absolutely no indication in his voice that he was under duress. He'd been talking intensely but quietly. Had had time to give me detailed directions. Someone other than he had parked the vehicle here.

And Hy...?

No time to speculate. The Rover was only fifty yards away, and I had a key—

Right. In my purse, back at the car.

So maybe the Rover wasn't locked. I could run over there, take refuge, look for evidence of what had happened to Hy.

I studied the house and surrounding terrain, then ran for the Rover.

A flat, cracking sound came from somewhere far beyond the house. Oh, God—rifle shot! Another.

Instinctively I dropped to the ground, scrabbled toward the car on my hands and knees. When I reached the Rover, I rolled under it.

A second shot reverberated faintly through the tall trees. Then silence.

CRAIG MORLAND

Again he was looking at the Andersen Associates appeal file, this time searching for a dimly remembered name. He had a growing feeling that there was information in it that would shed light on the current case. Maybe not a direct link, but a similarity...

Intuition worked in unknowable ways. You either had it or you didn't, and nobody who did knew exactly how to make it work for them. You tried certain tacks: at the Bureau, Craig had seen agents playing solitaire to loosen up their minds; others worked out, ran, watched crap TV to the point of numbness. A fair number drank, and if they came up with solutions to their cases, no questions were asked. His method, when there was nothing left to do in the field, was to immerse himself in files—related, nonrelated, it didn't matter. There were gems lying around everywhere; all you had to do was find them and pick them up.

Halfway into the much-read file he found one: the transcript of Shar's interview with Josh Ramsey, the Seattle blogger who would be testifying for Andersen in the appeal.

"This guy from a government agency called TRIAD came to see me. Handed me the information about Andersen and paid me to publish it...No, he didn't give me his full name, just said to call him J.T."

Craig flipped through the pages. No additional mention of

TRIAD or J.T., just more interviews with Ramsey, now claiming it was Stanley Hurd—the chief witness for the prosecution and former Andersen employee—who had given him the story. Hurd maintained his innocence.

TRIAD had probably bought Ramsey's silence.

Superclandestine or rogue CIA department concerned with maintaining the positions of the rich and powerful. Ruining Andersen Associates for reasons of their own. Agency still in operation, but no longer sanctioned by the government.

An interesting example: what if some person or group had gathered information against another contractor TRIAD supported? Or TRIAD itself? Was going to go public with the information? If TRIAD found out, they would take immediate steps to stop the person, suppress the information.

And how would they do that? Bait a hook and reel in the big-mouthed fish.

Craig picked up his phone and placed a call to Josh Ramsey.

TED SMALLEY

He'd sat in his car at the side of the road above Inverness for almost half an hour. At first he'd stared anxiously at the place where Shar had disappeared into the shadows. Then he'd tried to distract himself by thinking silk. Suddenly the whole subject of fashion statements bored him.

Next he thought about the folks at the agency. Craig, who was going through hell. Thelia, doggedly running her searches. Mick, similarly driven. Patrick, plugging information into his flow charts and connecting facts and figures.

Ted didn't know how Patrick managed to be a single father and put in long hours at the agency as well. He himself was adept at multitasking, but he couldn't imagine raising two children on his own. But Patrick loved those kids and was committed to them for the long haul.

As for himself, he was glad he didn't have offspring. He had enough young people to advise—or maybe lead astray. Habiba Hamid, adopted daughter of his old friends Anne-Marie Altman and Hank Zahn. Julia Rafael's son, Tonio. Thelia Chen's girls and Patrick's boys. And the younger Little Savages.

He was up to his ass in children.

And up to his ass in worry.

Hours had turned into days and Adah was still missing. Everybody was doing what they could, but with so little result. And that friend of Shar's—Piper Quinn—he couldn't imagine what had happened to her. Truthfully, he didn't care. He hadn't known Piper, and she was the reason for Adah's disappearance.

His resentment of Piper was coupled with guilt, but if he could have miraculously transported Adah back to them, he would have relinquished Piper in a heartbeat.

He wondered how Shar would feel about that.

The sky was lightening now, and he could see the road Shar had gone up more clearly. Unpaved, rutted, foliage deep to either side. Anxiety overwhelmed him again. She and Hy should have come down by now.

Unless...

He put down the window on his side. Chill morning, mist still hovering. Birdsong from the trees. And then—

Sharp, cracking sound from up there on the hill.

A gunshot! Jesus!

After a frozen moment he reached for his phone in slow motion. Called the agency. Craig picked up.

Ted tried to explain the situation, but his words sounded garbled, even to himself.

"Slow down," Craig said. "Take a deep breath and tell me exactly what happened."

He sucked in air, then gave a rambling but coherent recitation.

"How long to get to Inverness?" Craig asked him.

"This time of day, going against traffic, maybe an hour and a half."

"We don't have that much time. RI has a chopper, don't they?"

"One, over in Oakland at general aviation."

"And a pilot?"

"There's a pilot on call. But I don't know his name—"

"Find out—RI is a twenty-four-seven operation. Get hold of him and tell him to meet me at the airfield." Craig hung up.

Ted went into his efficient mode and made the arrangements.

One request of Shar's that he wouldn't honor: he wasn't going back to the pier till he knew what had happened up there.

ADAH JOSLYN

Her fingers ached and she felt a nasty little pinch in her neck, but she kept working on the new potential weapon she'd thought of. Fashioning the underwire from her bra into a garrote. It wasn't as easy as she'd thought because the flexible wire was coated with a slippery plastic, but it was coming along nicely.

Of course, when her captor came she'd have to be alert and in a position to get the thing around his neck. She'd figure out the logistics later, and being on guard was no problem. Not now, with rage fueling her.

Got it! Manageable and lethal.

She set the garrote down, then stood and began stretching exercises to keep her muscles toned and her body limber. Followed those with more serious calisthenics that raised her heartbeat and invigorated her. All the time she listened for any sound, trying to sense any change in the atmosphere that would tell her someone had arrived here. Wherever *here* was...

Her self-protective mode operated separately from her emotions, however. Soon she was exercising in cadence to a single word: Craig.

Craig, Craig, Craig...

If she got out of this situation alive—and she damn well would—she'd agree to set a date for their marriage. The hell with her reservations about joining his Waspy East Coast clan; maybe they'd do her a favor and disown him. But that wasn't fair: she'd never met the Morlands, only heard about them from Craig's biased viewpoint, and weren't children always critical of their parents?

Lord knew she'd repeatedly informed Barbara and Rupert about how much embarrassment they'd caused her over the years with their commie-pinko-liberal antics. The time they'd chained themselves to a flagpole to support a longshoremen's strike. The day Barbara—no longer young or firm—had joined a nude-in at the beach with Women for Peace and been photographed from a low-flying airplane. Rupert standing, clothed—thank God— entirely in red, on the city hall steps with a banner that said that the defeat of a rent-control measure was fascism.

They'd both made the evening news. Most of the neighborhood kids on Red Hill had eccentric parents, but none so publicly weird as hers. Most of the kids on Red Hill didn't have ambitions to be cops.

But now, released from the conformity of the very young, she was as proud of her folks as a daughter could be. Maybe they hadn't changed the world, maybe they'd been publicly viewed as ridiculous characters but, by God, they'd cared and tried to do something about society's ills.

Craig's parents would probably find them quaint and foolish and out of touch with the times, but so what? Maybe they'd learn something from the Joslyns.

And maybe if Craig's parents accepted their union, it would heal the rancor between them and their son.

Adah began cooling-down exercises, but his name continued to reverberate.

Craig, Craig, Craig . . .

SHARON McCONE

As soon as the echoes from the shots had subsided, I drew the Magnum, scrabbled out from under Hy's Rover, and again took shelter in the pines. My heart was pounding, my right shoulder hurt where I'd gone down on it. And I was suddenly wickedly thirsty.

Scanning the surrounding terrain I saw no one. Heard nothing. Even the cries of the birds were still. No breeze, no motion. Stationary gray mist. A chill in the air, and the acrid smell of blue gum eucalyptus in my nostrils.

This might have been a place where no one existed except for me. Where Hy didn't exist anymore...

No. Our connection was still there, alive and humming. I gave myself over to it, letting it guide me like an airport's flashing green-and-white beacon.

Out from under the pines, creeping low and across to the house.

Up to peer quickly through a window. Living room, disordered, two dirty glasses and three wine bottles on the coffee table. Television on but muted, one of those early-morning shows. No sign of anybody. Although the room was disordered, it didn't seem as if anything more violent had gone on in there but a bout of drinking.

I slipped around the house, cloaked by the misty dawn

shadows, and went up on a sagging deck that extended the width of the rear wall. The yard around it was weedy and gopher-holed, surrounded by some kind of bushes choked with dead blackberry vines. Behind it rose pine-covered hills whose tops were tinged with pink from the rising sun.

A crookedly hung screen door leading into the house stood open.

I steadied my weapon and moved toward it, skirting an old rusted barbecue and shabby folding chairs. Stopped just outside and listened.

Silence. The silence of an empty place.

The door opened into an old-style kitchen: olive-green Formica counters, chipped porcelain double sink, ancient fridge and range. A long table with benches to either side took up much of the space. And on the far wall, next to a hallway, was a gun cabinet. Its door stood ajar, and the space for one rifle was empty.

The birdsongs had gradually resumed. A crow soared over the pines, and its sudden caw made me jerk. I gathered myself and stepped into the house. Made my way silently through the kitchen.

Two front rooms, the one I'd glimpsed through its window and a bedroom, sparsely furnished, with a mattress on the floor. The bedclothes were disordered and looked unclean. An odor rose from them: rank, fetid.

Back outside. I then saw that the double doors to the shed Hy's Rover was parked in front of were pushed out, boards broken. I went over, found a padlocked hasp had been broken loose. In the shadowy interior I saw jumbled tools.

Someone had been imprisoned here and broken out.

Hy.

Behind me twigs snapped. I caught a glimpse of motion at the edge of the pines. I ducked behind the shed and waited.

A man's figure emerged from the trees. A man cradling a rifle. He moved unhurriedly, as if he'd completed a job and had nothing else to do.

HY RIPINSKY

He lay at the bottom of the ravine, ferns and vines and scrub trees sheltering him. No sound came from above. The shooter must've been sure of his aim, not to have come over here to make sure his target was dead. Either that, or he was incredibly stupid. Probably the latter. Confining a prisoner in a toolshed with easy means of escape was a dumb-ass thing to do.

His shoulder hurt like hell. He lay still a while longer, mentally beating himself up for having gotten caught and then shot. Then he sat up, and after his vision cleared and his head stopped swimming, gingerly probed the wound. Not too much blood, and he could move his arm—the bullet had passed straight through without severing an artery or clipping a bone.

He put a finger into the hole where his shirt was torn, ripped off a strip, and fashioned a makeshift bandage.

He'd been hit before, a flesh wound in Mexico that he quickly recovered from, and another time when a hostage taker he'd been negotiating with had gotten nervous and fired a round. That had been bad: a slug that cracked a rib and narrowly missed his vital organs. Two of his backup negotiators had shot the guy and saved the hostage, and there'd been a medevac chopper on site in minutes. Once aboard, the EMTs had administered meds, and the pain had subsided, and within days he'd forgotten its intensity. Until now.

This wasn't as bad, but today there would be no chopper.

McCone, where are you? Please not anywhere near that stupid asshole with the rifle.

Fear for her tightened his chest. He thought of how far she'd come, how much she'd struggled. And how in their last couple of months together he'd been so pissed at her. For simply being herself, goddammit.

The sky above the trees showed sunlight breaking through the haze. Time to try to find her and get help for himself, in that order.

SHARON McCONE

I crouched behind the broken-down deck and watched the man cross to the house. He was large and tall with longish blond hair held back by a thick leather band. Boots, jeans, a Western-style shirt under a fringed jacket. Maybe around forty, judging from the lines on his face. Tough looking.

A dreadful, empty feeling washed over me, followed by a numbing chill. My limbs stopped functioning, and my vocal chords wouldn't work. I felt like some biblical character who was turned to stone, or to a pillar of salt. I could hear the birds and the rustling of branches and dimly see the pines, but otherwise I was as close to the locked-in state as I'd been when I crashed at Brandt Institute and was rushed to SF General to have the crippling bullet removed from my brain.

The slamming of the screen door as the man went inside jerked me out of my paralysis. I forced myself to focus on what the man would do next. Probably he'd clean the gun. Or he might just lock it in the cabinet. No, he'd be thorough—and that gave me time to plan.

What about Hy? He could be anywhere in these hills, dead or wounded. I had no way of knowing—but this man did.

I moved up onto the deck, peered through the door. He was at the table cleaning his rifle. I flattened against the side wall. Shortly I heard his chair scrape and then a door clicked shut—the gun cabinet. Footsteps moved toward the front of the house, into the room where he'd earlier been drinking wine. Noise from there: the morning news on the previously muted TV, turned up loud. The familiar voice of the ABC anchor was talking about the Morell Associates plane crash: "All three passengers and the pilot were killed when the aircraft struck an isolated slope in the Rockies...."

He sounds almost pleased. The media loves to serve disaster up to the public.

I slipped along the hall, holding the Magnum in both hands. Paused beside the open door to the front room, then peered around the jamb. The blond man was pouring what was left in a bottle of wine into one of the empty glasses. I came around the doorjamb, gun extended.

"Put the bottle down and your hands up."

His head jerked and the bottle fell from his hand, smashing the glass into which he'd been pouring.

"Get up!"

He slowly stood.

"Facedown on the floor. Spread your legs, cross your wrists behind you."

"Who the hell—?"

"Go on, do it!"

He hesitated, and then complied.

I knelt on his back, the Magnum's muzzle pressed hard against his neck. "That's my husband's vehicle in your yard. Where is he?"

"I dunno what you're talking about. It's my—"

"*Where is he?*"

Long silence. "In...the woods."

"Did you kill him?"

No response.

I gouged him with the .357. "*Did you?*"

No response.

I could have shot him right then, but if I did I might never find Hy.

Angrily I yanked off the leather headband, ripping out a few strands of hair in the process. Switched the gun to my left hand and used my right to bind his wrists. Jerked the band till it was tight and tied a knot one-handed.

"This is trespassing, false imprisonment—"

"Shut up!"

"You're not going to shoot me, lady. I shot that guy in self-defense."

"Shot him? You mean killed him?"

No response.

"If he's dead, so are you. You won't be the first person I've killed."

Silence. Then: "You're Ripinsky's wife? That McCone woman."

"Yeah, I'm that McCone woman. Now get up."

"I can't."

"Yeah, you can." I grabbed him by his belt, pulled him to his feet, steadied him. Then I marched him outside, through the yard, and into the woods.

CRAIG MORLAND

The RI chopper pilot had located the area where Ted had said he'd taken Shar by his air nav device even before Craig arrived at North Field. Now as they crossed over the Golden Gate, heading for west Marin, Craig's phone rang. He said to the pilot through their linked headsets, "Okay to take this?"

"Sure. It's not going to screw up the radio on this baby."

Mick. "God, this reception is terrible."

"I'm still on the chopper."

"Well, listen up. I just caught a major break. Remember I thought that sketch you brought me was familiar? There's a good reason. Although he's altered his appearance, it's Specialist Ryan Middleton of the U.S. Marine Corps."

"Middleton? Piper Quinn's husband? He's dead."

"Reportedly dead. Mistakes happen."

And sometimes they happen deliberately. "Refresh me: what was Middleton's specialty?"

"Tactical intelligence officer."

"Someone who owned a great deal of confidential and sensitive information."

"Right."

"How was he supposedly killed?"

"Terrorist bombing in Mosul. Official report said all that was found were body parts and his dog tags."

"Dog tags can be switched."

"Right."

Craig was replaying his conversation with Josh Ramsey, the Seattle blogger.

Okay, yeah, this J.T. from TRIAD did pay me to put out the information on Andersen Associates. I told Ms. McCone about him in our initial interview, but then I got a second visit from J.T. and a lot more cash to keep quiet.

No, I haven't heard from them again. Don't expect to. These agencies, what they do is scatter stuff among bloggers like me; if I reported on too much, I'd eventually become an unreliable source.

Why did I do it? I needed the money.

Who do I think they'll approach next? Do you know how many people are out there in the blogosphere?

So, Craig thought, a quasi-government agency wants to plant a story, and there're a lot of hungry people out there hunched over their keyboards just waiting for a chance at a big score. And Ryan Middleton had access to many kinds of information. What if he'd somehow faked his death and slipped back into the country to capitalize on whatever he'd learned? Was going to go public through an intermediary for a hefty price?

Craig could understand why Middleton might have done it: after years in intelligence with the marines he'd probably seen cover-ups and profit-grabbing beyond most people's comprehension. Middleton's wife had served him with divorce papers, he'd lost faith in the corps he'd served, maybe lost any moral base. Craig had had a crisis like that before he left the Bureau. He knew how betrayal by the institutions one believed in could eat away at a person's soul.

Piper? Snatched in a quasi-government operation. Not dead, he thought. Middleton had been asking about her, probably had been the one seen "casing" her building. Maybe had been the man Craig had chased down the alley. Whoever had her was holding her as a lure for her husband.

Conjecture, he thought. But it all fit and it had to be right.

"Keep working on TRIAD, Mick."

"Will do."

The pilot had cut back on power and they were descending. He began a series of sweeps of the wooded terrain, spotlights illuminating trees, roofs, and clearings. After a moment, he said, "Mr. Morland, we're over the property you're looking for. I just spotted a man and a woman crossing into the woods behind."

Hy and Shar? Or Shar and the man Hy had been running the surveillance on?

Craig looked down but all he could see was forest and a couple of ramshackle buildings.

"Did it look like she's under duress?"

"I don't think so, sir. The man was leading and it looked like his hands were clasped behind his back."

"Put us down as close as you can to where you saw them."

ADAH JOSLYN

Her captor hadn't come back. She knew from the way her stomach was rumbling that it was long after dark. Good God, was he going to leave her here to starve?

Every muscle in her body ached from exercising, but in a good way. Her mind had gone blank during the repetitive motions. For a while she'd tried to amuse herself with reciting favorite poems: William Butler Yeats.

Earth in beauty dressed
Awaits returning spring
All true love must die
Alter, at best, into some lesser thing
Prove that I lie.

Yeah, Yeats was a melancholy fellow. Come to think of it, most of the Irish poets were not a bundle of laughs. But, then, the last line of the poem suggested a challenge.

Everything in Adah's life had been a challenge. From the playground bully to the rigors of a strict, private, socialist-oriented school, to her parents' opposition to her going to the police academy. The academy itself, and the department: being elevated to a high position too soon, the poster-girl treatment and resentment of her fellow officers.

Normally such reflections would have overwhelmed her, sent her spiraling into despair. Now she used them to keep her spirits up.

Prove that I lie.

You betcha.

She decided to practice using the garrote.

SHARON McCONE

I heard the chopper come whirring overhead as I prodded the blond man toward the trees. Going to fly right over the property, and if it was a flyover by strangers I didn't want them to see a woman with a gun herding a bound man. He went easily; he didn't want to be seen either.

It wasn't a flyover—the chopper was descending, probably to land on the open ground behind the house. Above the trees I could make out the familiar number on its fuselage. It belonged to RI.

Huge relief. I told the blond man to turn around, hurried him out of the woods into the clearing.

The chopper landed, its rotors stirring up clouds of dust and pine needles. A figure got out of the chopper and ran toward me. Craig.

"Where's Hy?" he called, as the pilot shut the chopper down.

"This guy is taking me to him. And he'd better be alive when we find him. How did you know to come here?"

"Ted called me." Craig came up, looked closely at the man's face. "Who is he?"

I hadn't even thought to ask his name, so great was my anxiety about Hy. Now I had to prod him twice before he said sullenly, "Bob Samson."

Craig said, "Who do you work for? Morell Associates?"

"Yeah. I'm Kurt Morell's nephew, and I want to know—"

"Save it. Let's get going." To Craig I added, "Talk about hiring the weak link in the family; this guy is as inept as they come."

Samson said, "Fuck you, lady," but he moved when I prodded him forward.

The trail—probably a deer track—led under the pines where the ground was slick with decaying needles. After a few zigs and zags, Samson veered off and we followed a narrower trail through thick branches and scrub vegetation. None of us spoke. After a ways we came out into a clearing.

Samson stopped. "Down there," he said, motioning with his head. "In the ravine."

"Watch him," I said to Craig. I stuffed my gun into my belt and hurried ahead to the ravine.

It was steep-sided and rocky, with a trickle of a stream at its bottom. There were scuff marks and dislodged stones on its lip— probably where Hy had gone over. But there was no sign of him below. I scanned the ground to either side, then scrambled down for a closer look. Blood smears marked the spot where he'd fallen. Hurt then, but still alive.

I went up and down the ravine, calling for him, but he didn't answer. Finally I climbed back up top, where Craig stood guard over Samson. Took my gun from my belt and shoved the muzzle into Samson's belly.

"He's not there. You've got ten seconds to tell me where he is."

Samson went pale. "Lady, I don't know where he is. Last I saw of him he went over the edge. I told you, he fired at me first, it was my life or his."

"No way—he wasn't armed. And I heard the shots. Two, close together, from a rifle, not a handgun."

"He had a rifle—"

"The hell he did. He doesn't own one. Why didn't you check to see if he was alive?"

"Because I knew he wasn't. I'm a crack shot."

God, what an idiot! Staring down at a loaded handgun and boasting!

"Just leave the body where it fell, right? Like a dead animal for the scavengers to pick over."

"What else would I do with it?" My finger tightened on the trigger. Then I relaxed it. I'd had enough of killing years ago, and we needed Samson to tell us what he'd done with Adah.

Instead I jabbed him once more, hard. "You are one worthless, pathetic son of a bitch."

Craig said, "Hy must be around here somewhere. If he's hurt, he couldn't have gone far."

"I'll hunt for him. You stay here with ... that."

"Just what I was about to suggest. He's going to tell me where Adah is—one way or another."

HY RIPINSKY

It seemed like hours ago that he had pulled himself over the edge of the ravine and lain on his good side, panting. The woods were still, although during his struggle to climb up he'd heard a chopper hovering, maybe landing somewhere nearby. Did Morell Associates have a helicopter? He wasn't sure. Their offices were downscale, but low overhead in that department could support a small fleet of aircraft.

He'd flown choppers. They were legal at low altitudes, and you could take them lower illegally. But a pilot's eyes could see only so far. If he kept to the cover of the trees and moved slowly, he might make it to the highway or some secondary road—

Stealthy motion in the brush some distance away, but too damn close for a man with a bullet hole in his shoulder.

The shooter coming back to finish him off? Another Morell op?

He could slide back into the ravine, but the noise might draw attention to him, and he'd be an easy target down there. He could try to hide, but with the morning light shining through the trees he didn't see any likely places. He could still try for the highway—

No, he couldn't. The wound had started bleeding again after his climb up the slope. He was starting to feel light-headed, weak, thirsty....

McCone, he thought, *where are you? Hope to God this maniac hasn't gotten his hands on you. No, you came out here primed for trouble. You're too smart to get caught like I did. I used to be smart, maybe I'm losing it.*

The sounds in the woods were closer now.

He looked around for something he could use to defend himself.

SHARON McCONE

I followed the ravine for about twenty yards, calling out to Hy and getting no response. Finally, then, I saw disturbed rocks, gouges in the earth—footholds. Nearby I found freshly disturbed marks in the spongy earth and followed the trail into the trees, batting branches and vines out of my way, shouting.

No response.

"Ripinsky!"

Nothing.

"Ripinsky!"

Then his weak voice came through the trees to my right.

"Over here."

He's alive! I knew it, I knew it!

"Where?" I called, my voice shaking.

"Not far, big Doug fir splintered by lightning."

I hurried toward the source of his voice. The tree was huge, the splintered section lying between two other firs. Hy was behind it, on his side. He was pale and sweating. How the hell had he made it this far?

I checked his pulse, peered into his eyes. The pulse was thready, his pupils widely dilated with pain and residual shock. "Where're you hit?"

"My shoulder. You okay?"

"Yes. Craig's here too."

He let out a ragged breath. "So that chopper was RI's. What about the asshole who shot me? He get away?"

"No, I got him and Craig's questioning him. I'll explain later. Let me see your wound."

He'd torn away his shirt and made a bandage. The edges of the bullet hole were ragged but mostly clean and, when I gingerly probed the other side, I was relieved to find them the same.

"Doesn't look so bad. Bullet seems to've gone straight through."

"Some antiseptic, stitches, and pain meds, and I'll be fine."

"You're lucky," I told him.

"Lucky you found me. Not lucky to be shot by some nut ball who shouldn't've been able to make me in the first place."

"It's not your fault."

"Was stupid. Who else's fault but mine?"

"Okay, you did something stupid. Who hasn't?" I eased him into a sitting position, his back against my chest; put my arms around him. He smelled of sweat, and blood, and of something else—familiar, pleasant—that was his scent alone. I closed my eyes, felt tears on my cheeks. This wasn't one of those times when I was crying reflexively.

After a minute or so, I asked, "Can you walk?"

"Give me a bit."

"The shooter said you were in the ravine."

"Crawled up and took cover here."

"He also claimed he shot you in self-defense."

"Crock of shit. You know I wasn't armed." Long pause. "I think I can get up and walk now."

I got his arm around my shoulders and wrapped mine around his waist and we started back out of the woods. I felt a searing pain in my back from the unaccustomed activity, ignored it.

"Adah," he said. "You found her?"

"Not yet. We'll get it out of Samson—that's his name, Bob Samson—where he stashed her. In the meantime, the chopper can take you to Marin General. We'd better have a cover story ready. They'll have to file a police report, and we don't want the law to know what went on up here."

"Right. Hunting accident?"

"It's not hunting season."

"So I'm a poacher."

"How about just saying you were cleaning your rifle and it went off?"

"Lame. Besides, they'd want to see the rifle, check its registration."

"Unknown assailant shot you while you were hiking in the woods?"

"Where in the woods? The National Seashore isn't open to visitors this early in the day, and on private property I'd be trespassing." He paused. "Hey, fuzzy thinking on my part—the chopper pilot used to be an EMT, and we keep a first aid kit on board."

I hesitated. "You trust him to deal with a gunshot wound?"

"He has before. Besides, it's only a flesh wound."

"But there could be complications—"

"I'll see the doctor that RI uses for situations like this when I get back to the city. He won't ask questions or report it."

"Okay. It's a ways to the chopper, but you can lean on Craig while I watch Samson. You want to rest first?"

"I just want to get the hell out of here."

"You in much pain?"

"Bearable, now that you're with me."

CRAIG MORLAND

Bob Samson wasn't admitting anything, even with Craig's weapon under his nose. He looked sullen and spat on the ground a couple of times. Craig was out of patience with him.

He said, "One more time—where are Piper Quinn and Adah Joslyn? I'll use this gun, goddamn you."

Silence.

"Either you or TRIAD snatched them from Quinn's building on Tenth Avenue."

"I don't know no TRIAD."

"J. T. Verke, then."

"Who?"

"Rogue ex-CIA. A very dangerous man to deal with, Samson."

"I didn't deal with nobody."

"Your uncle and his partners did—look what happened to them."

Silence.

"They can find you, Samson. There're hundreds of ways they can take you out."

Samson was sweating now. He looked down, shuffled his feet.

"Even if you never get on a plane again, there're always car bombs. Incendiary devices under your house. A drive-by shooting. Poison in your In-N-Out burger."

Samson's Adam's apple bobbed.

"I imagine you'd be eligible for the witness protection program if you come clean on this."

"Oh sure—live in some shithole as somebody else. You don't get it—Morell Associates is mine, now that my uncle's toast. I got my life right here."

"Not if the office blows up when you unlock the door some morning."

"Ah, shit." He scuffled on the ground some more. "I never did that much, and I never snatched nobody. All's I did was find a place to stash 'em and take 'em food."

"What place? Where?"

Silence.

Craig slapped his cheek with the gun barrel. *"Where?"*

"I don't remember."

"Bullshit."

"They've been moved. I'm out of it now. End of story."

"Who took them? TRIAD?" Craig moved as if to slap him again, and Samson flinched.

"Yeah. They hired my uncle's firm to clean up this building on Tenth Avenue."

"Why'd they take the women?"

"Trying to use the Quinn broad to lure some guy who has information they want. The other was snooping around, saw one of the TRIAD agents, so they took her too."

"Who's this guy they're after?"

"Marine intelligence. Went AWOL in Iraq under somebody else's name."

Piper Quinn's husband.

Keeping his voice steady, Craig asked, "You say your uncle's firm did the cleanup on Tenth Avenue?"

"Yeah."

"And where did you hold the women?"

"This place my uncle's company runs security on. Verke told him where."

"What place?"

"Doesn't matter. They're gone now."

"Gone *where*?"

"I don't know!"

Craig heard sounds in the trees nearby, then Shar's voice called, "Hey, Craig, look who I found." A moment later she came into view, Hy hobbling beside her with their arms around each other. Hy looked pale, and Shar didn't look much better. All this physical exertion couldn't be good for her.

"Ripinsky—you all right, man?"

"I'll live—no thanks to this asshole."

Shar said to Craig, "You help Hy to the chopper—the pilot used to be an EMT. I'll watch Samson. He tell you anything?"

"Some. Not enough."

"Adah? Piper?"

"Lying bastard claims he doesn't know where they are."

Craig took over support of Hy, while Shar held her weapon on Samson. The four of them made their way through the woods to the clearing. At the chopper, Shar and Hy and the pilot conferred for a moment. When she came back to where Craig stood with Samson, Craig related the rest of what Samson had told him.

"Okay," she said, facing Samson. "This place Morell Associates runs security on—where is it?"

"Like I told this guy, it don't matter. They've been moved."

"Where to?"

"Nobody told me."

"TRIAD—how did they contact you?"

"This J. T. Verke came into the office, flashing a lot of cash."

"And you did what?"

"Standard cleanup on the apartment building."

"How many tenants were living there?"

"Just the woman. Verke was sort of camping out there."

"Again, where did you hold Adah and Piper?"

Headshake.

"Fast-forward a little. Who was the woman who visited you here last night?"

"Some skank I met in this pickup joint in San Rafael."

"Her name?"

"Who knows? That kind of place, you don't bother with names."

"The place's name?"

"I don't remember."

"When did you meet her? Last night?"

"No. Three, four nights ago. Last night she just showed up here. That didn't sit well with me, but I let her stay awhile."

"Ms. McCone," the pilot called out from the chopper. "I need to speak with you for a minute."

Concern registered on Shar's face. She turned and hurried over there. Craig watched her go.

In that instant of inattention, Samson lunged at him and sent him reeling. Before Craig could regain his equilibrium, Samson head-butted him in the stomach and knocked him sprawling backward on his ass. As he struggled up, gasping for breath, he saw Samson crashing away into the woods.

A handgun cracked from the direction of the chopper. Shar had seen what happened, fired a warning shot. No way she'd shoot to kill their only witness.

But Samson didn't stop. A couple of seconds later he vanished among the trees.

Shar started running after him. Craig sucked in air, cursing himself, and joined the pursuit.

Their convergent paths brought them together at the edge of the woods. Craig could hear Samson stumbling through the undergrowth somewhere ahead of them, the snapping sound of a branch breaking off.

"Bastard! I only took my eyes off him for a second."

"Don't worry, he can't get far with his hands tied."

They plunged ahead, following the noises as best they could. But they still couldn't spot Samson in the murky darkness.

"Dammit." Craig panted. "He knows these woods a lot better than we do. If he finds a place to hole up…"

"He won't. We'll get him."

More thrashing, snapping sounds, coming from off to their left now. They veered that way. The soft earth was slippery here; Shar, in the lead, nearly lost her footing and had to grab at a fir bole to keep herself from falling. Her breathing was heavy and irregular. Craig moved to steady her, but she shook him off.

She's going to do herself damage. Maybe have a relapse—or die.

Ahead, the trees thinned and the terrain rose above a clearing that looked like a small amphitheater. Samson was at the far end, struggling to climb to higher ground beyond. Craig yelled at him to stop, but it was a waste of breath. Samson lurched sideways and kept going.

They were halfway across the clearing when Samson reached the top of the rise. For an instant he was backlit by a shaft of sunlight; then he staggered forward and disappeared on the other side.

Craig pushed around Shar and increased his stride, urgency making him careless of his footing now. Shar was trailing him on the rising ground when they heard a sudden yell, then a thudding noise that cut off the outcry.

"Christ," Craig said, "what was that?"

"Sounded like he ran into something."

Craig pounded up to where they could see what lay behind the rise, Shar climbing more slowly. The terrain sloped downward again, sharply, the ground covered with ferns, vines, and a tangled deadfall.

At the base of a thick-trunked pine near the deadfall, Samson lay in a twisted heap, unmoving.

Craig ran ahead, knelt beside him with a sick, sinking sensation in the pit of his stomach. Samson must have tried to avoid the deadfall, tripped, lost his balance, and careened sideways. With his hands tied behind him, he'd had no way to stop himself and he'd hit the tree head-on. There was no need to feel for a pulse.

Shar came up beside him. "Dead?"

"Broken neck, goddammit. Snapped like a twig."

And there goes my last link to Adah.

ADAH JOSLYN

She was starving, her body racked by alternating cold and hot spells. Getting sick. Going to die alone on this filthy quilt, and maybe nobody she loved would ever know what happened to her.

Many cases like that when she was on Missing Persons, before she transferred to Homicide. If they didn't turn up within the first twenty-four hours, forty-eight tops, you could pretty much consider them gone.

Children missing, wives missing, husbands missing, friends missing. Media exposure. Nutcases coming out of whatever strange universe they dwelled in to give false confessions and false leads. A sighting here, another there—most unverifiable. Relatives begging for new developments, their voices made more dull and hopeless by the passage of time.

The ones that really bothered her were the kids; husbands and wives and friends had a tendency to disappear voluntarily. But the kids—innocent, easily duped by strangers, snatched, abused, tortured, killed. They'd haunted her on the job. Haunted her still. Every so often, even after she was promoted to Homicide, she'd pull up their files, hoping some detail from the past would connect with the present.

Adah remembered working San Francisco sightings on the Jaycee Lee Dugard case; it was an exception. An eleven-year-old girl had gone missing from her neighborhood in South Lake

Tahoe eighteen years ago. She was found last summer—a grown woman living in a shed in the yard of the house belonging to the couple who had taken her. Of course, she'd lost her childhood, had two children of her own fathered by the kidnapper. Lots of problems with adjustment there, but still she'd come home.

All too often they didn't come back. Then there was the horrible, grief-filled closure: a body that had been found under a freeway overpass twenty years before identified by the newish science of DNA; a sudden confession from a murderer brought in on minor charges; a father of one of the missing cracking under pressures related to his present-day life and admitting to a crime against his own flesh and blood.

Such closures were bad, but not knowing was a hundred times worse. The harshest pain was of those who waited throughout their lifetimes, who died without ever knowing what had happened to the lost. Mothers and fathers living out their old age in silence and resignation. Husbands or wives putting everything on hold in the hopes their spouse would return. Friends searching every crowd for the missing one's face. Uncertainty, frustration, constant anxiety—and every phone call or knock at the door threatening to smash their worlds forever.

Adah didn't want that to happen to Craig, to her parents and friends.

Dammit, she wouldn't let it happen! She *wouldn't*.

CRAIG MORLAND

They stood looking down at what was left of Bob Samson. Craig felt a despairing emptiness.

Worse than when he and his colleagues had found the body of the kidnapped seven-year-old son of a diplomat in a junkyard in Maryland. Worse than when a fellow field agent's head had exploded in a hail of bullets from the semi-automatic of a bank robber in rural West Virginia. Worse, even, than when his younger sister had drowned in the Atlantic off the Outer Banks of North Carolina.

The first two tragedies had been horrible, but they went with the job's territory. His sister—eighteen years younger than he, a change-of-life baby. Kristina was her name. She'd been only thirteen. Blonde curls, blue eyes, big smile, long, long legs. He'd loved her, but he'd hardly known her, having been mostly gone from home since her birth. That distance had allowed him to be strong for his grieving parents.

Who would be strong for him, now that he'd lost Adah?

Shar, apparently. She took his arm as the chopper lifted off, taking Hy back to the city. Squeezed it tightly, then laced her fingers through his.

"We are not giving up yet," she said.

The hell with not giving up. It was over. For a savage moment he wanted to smack Shar, ream her out for ever bringing Piper Quinn into their lives.

Shar's eyes met his, something dangerous and ugly glittering deep within them. She understood and shared what he was feeling.

She said, "The chopper pilot'll come back after we search Samson's cabin. In the meantime, will you please climb down there and remove the headband from that son of a bitch's wrists. If he's found, it'll look like an accidental death. If not, let the buzzards and coyotes have his remains—as he was willing to let them have Hy's."

SHARON McCONE

Craig and I began a careful search of Samson's cabin, looking for anything that would tell us where he'd taken Adah. In the kitchen I found Hy's BlackBerry, wallet, and keys. I pocketed them and continued searching, trying to concentrate on every object I looked at or handled, but my body ached badly and my thoughts kept straying to the possibilities.

Bob Samson had told Craig that TRIAD was holding Piper as a lure for her supposedly dead husband, Ryan Middleton. Quasi-government agency. If they wanted to reel him in, Piper would have to be at a location Middleton knew of and would gravitate to.

But wouldn't he suspect a trap? Maybe, but the lure of Piper might be stronger.

Why? She'd served divorce papers on him. He'd apparently faked his own death and escaped Iraq with classified information.

A smoke screen? Some political ploy they'd gone in on together?

No. Piper wasn't a political animal. She'd told me she hadn't even voted in the last election.

Well, a monetary scam, then.

Wrong again. Piper didn't need money, had never shown the slightest inclination toward acquiring material possessions. Just the reverse—she was generous to a fault.

So she probably wasn't aware Middleton had survived the suicide bomb blast. Why should she be? His remains—or those of a man identified by his dog tags—had been sent back and interred in Colma. His personal effects had been returned to her. She'd been recovering from a crippling accident, which had left her life forever changed. The part of it that had belonged to Ryan Middleton was as dead as he supposedly was.

But not for Middleton.

My head ached and my eyes felt like I'd been in a sandstorm. My husband had insisted on forgoing a trip to an emergency service and returning home after only the minimal first aid given him by the chopper pilot. I wasn't sure that I hadn't damaged my health with all that running in the woods. I'd watched a man die and—in spite of my bravado about letting the coyotes take care of his body—any death felt like a part of myself slipping away. And now I feared I'd never see Adah again.

I sat down on the lumpy, stained couch in the front room.

No tears, McCone. Be strong for Craig. Wasn't he strong for you when you were locked-in and helpless? Wasn't Adah? And everybody else?

Craig called to me from outside, where he'd gone to search Adah's Prius.

I dragged myself up from the couch and out the front door. He stood by the car, several keys attached to a blue plastic tag dangling from his hand.

"They were in the ashtray," he said.

TED SMALLEY

He'd finally driven back to the pier when he'd seen the RI chopper hover over and descend toward the property above Inverness. Now he was waiting to hear from Shar or Craig or Hy. He was jumpy from too much coffee and had been plaguing Neal, who had returned from his book-buying trip to the Pacific Northwest, with half-hour updates.

Down the catwalk, Mick was at his keyboard, probably also wired on too much coffee. Thelia was at hers, still trying for a hit on Adah's or Piper's credit cards. Patrick was busily plugging information into his damned flow charts.

Why didn't Patrick get a life? Ted wondered. He buried himself in those useless diagrams, except for when he was worrying about his kids. He'd recently told Ted that the boys weren't doing well in their Catholic school, and it must be the nuns' fault. The nuns weren't strict enough, Patrick claimed, not like they were in the scary old days of his youth when they'd loomed over you like big black birds ready to pick the flesh from your bones if you broke any of their thousands of rules.

Back in his youth, Ted thought. Yeah—all of twenty years ago.

Besides, one of those kids needed excess flesh removed.

Bad, Ted. Very bad.

He knew he was taking out his concern about Adah and Shar and Hy on the Neilan household. And he shouldn't be: Patrick was a good guy, and the kids would eventually turn out okay, as they tended to do when there was a concerned parent around.

Truth was, Ted felt swamped because there was nobody in the office who had any real authority. Derek would've been a steadying influence, but he was still in LA attending to family matters. Julia would've pitched in, probably taken over, but she wasn't due back from her vacation till Saturday. Ted had thought of asking Rae to come in and help out—she had a real intuitive talent, had to have since she wrote those crime novels. But he wasn't sure Shar would approve of him calling Rae, seeing as she hadn't been briefed on the current situation, and...

By the time Kendra came through the door, he knew he was mentally babbling to himself.

His Paragon of the Paper Clips set a little paper plate containing a croissant, a pat of butter, and a container of jam—strawberry, it looked like—in front of him. Hunger pangs instantly kicked in.

"You buy this?" he asked.

"No." She smiled—her little cynical quirk of the lips that hinted of a devilish sense of humor that she hadn't chosen to fully reveal in her ten months with the agency. "Friend of Mick's did. Tall blonde lady name of Alison, carrying a wicker basket. Came in here looking like Li'l Red Riding Hood, but I'm guessing she's the Big Bad Wolf in disguise and has her sights set on eatin' him up."

Ted buttered the croissant. "You don't like her?"

"I don't like her, I don't dislike her. I just think she's a tall blonde lady name of Alison with a wicker basket. And the breakfast things she delivered are great."

The phone rang. Kendra answered. "For you," she said. "Hy Ripinsky."

SHARON McCONE

One of the keys on the ring Craig had found looked as if it might fit a heavy-duty padlock. Another was a standard dead bolt type. Both newish. Two others, one small and one large, were old and tarnished. Pockmarked and crusty, the way the keys Hy and I kept at Touchstone got if we didn't occasionally treat them with WD-40.

The blue tag felt finger-worn and smooth to the touch. Faint broken lines showed where a number once had been, and when I held it up to the light and squinted I made out the numeral 6 and the letter C. Across the bottom was a faded pattern of flames, or perhaps a sunset.

Craig was watching me anxiously. "Mean anything to you?"

"Not really." I turned it over. The back was blank except for scratches. "You sure this doesn't belong to Adah?"

"I'd've noticed it if it was in the ashtray before. Adah usually keeps the case of whatever CD she's playing propped in there."

"And you haven't seen it at home? Say, on that rack with the key hooks by the front door?"

"Never." The word was sharpened by impatience, but I ignored it, reexamining the tag.

I said, "It could be to a hotel or motel room. A lot of the older places still haven't converted to key cards."

"If Samson stashed Adah someplace like that, she'd've figured a way out by now."

"Unless he's been sedating her."

"Even then, places like that are too public. People coming and going, curious about what's happening in the adjoining units. Besides, hotels and motels don't require that many keys."

"No."

"Shar." Now his voice crackled with impatience. "We're wasting time."

"I'll take the tag to Richman Labs, see if they can bring out the writing."

"Will they put a priority on it?"

"They'd damn well better; we send a lot of business their way. I'll call to alert them, and you call RI, ask for the chopper to come back for me. You take Hy's Rover down and park it someplace inconspicuous on the lower road. Then drive Adah's Prius back to the city. By the time you get to the pier, we may have something on her whereabouts."

ADAH JOSLYN

*F*ace *it, the only way you're getting out of here is by forcing that door.*

But with what? Not the underwire. It wasn't strong enough to move that dead bolt. And she'd been over the whole space exhaustively; all she'd come up with was a damned useless toilet bolt. She looked at it where it lay on the quilt, then flung it away into the bathroom.

Childish reaction, but a situation like this reduced you to that. Brought out all those resentments and fears and tantrums that stalked the terrain of the young and helpless. She had been a willful child, and when someone crossed her—a playmate in the schoolyard, a babysitter, her own parents—then watch out! Rage had been her favorite and usually most effective weapon.

As an adult she'd learned to control her temper and use anger sparingly, but in certain situations it had served her well. This was not one of those times. Aimless fury sapped your strength, made you careless, and could plunge you into despair. She needed to regroup, regain focus. But focus on what? Escape? She'd apparently exhausted all possibilities of that.

Actually the bolt wasn't completely useless. She could chip away at the doorjamb with it. But she'd need something thin and strong to slide into the hole she'd create and force the bolt and snap lock aside.

She'd make one more search.

Nothing in this room. She went into the bathroom, retrieved the bolt from the floor and stood still, looking around. Her eyes rested on the metal flashing from which the shower door had hung. It was coming loose from the rest of the enclosure.

She felt a rush of excitement. What she needed had been here all along, she just hadn't examined it closely enough.

She reached up and pried the flashing free. Carried it to the other room and began chiseling at the doorjamb. At first the noise unnerved her, but no one came to investigate. She tried prematurely to slip the flashing in beside the lock, but it wouldn't go, so she continued chipping. The wood was old and splintered easily.

Now that she was close to freeing the lock, her little prison had started to feel damn cozy to her. Variation of the Stockholm syndrome, she supposed: instead of bonding with her captor, she was bonding with this tiny squalid hole he'd stuffed her into.

She felt the bolt on the lock move slightly. Eased off on the pressure, then tore at it again.

I want out of here. I want an hour-long shower and clean clothes. I want the biggest steak and the richest zinfandel I can find. I want my cats. I want Craig. I want to get laid!

Another slight giving motion in the lock.

Maybe the steak and zin can wait till later. Cats and the clothes too. But not the shower.

And certainly not Craig!

Wait, what was that?

Voices.

She stopped gouging at the doorjamb to listen. The voices were faint, but audible over the dripping and creaking sounds she'd by now normalized. Above her? Below? Couldn't tell.

Somebody coming to kill me?

Somebody coming to save me?

The voices were louder now. Two men and a woman. Words mostly unclear, but emotionally charged.

Adah moved into a defensive stance and grabbed the garrote. If they were coming for her, she'd put up the fight of her life.

"...what've...done...?" First man.

"...gave...it." Woman.

First man: "...get back..."

"...kill..." Second man.

"No...!" Woman.

Second man: "...who..."

"Can't..." Woman.

"...have twelve hours..." First man.

Woman: "...can't..."

A scuffle. A thud. Pained scream from the woman.

"Let her alone, you bastard!" Second man, loud.

Silence, except for the woman's exhausted crying.

A shout: "What did you *do* with it?" First man.

Woman. "I won't—"

More scuffling noises, and then a gunshot, reverberating hollowly. Its sound and echoing vibrations defined her prison's space and shape. Adah closed her eyes and began visualizing her surroundings.

MICK SAVAGE

It was there, staring out at him from one of the obscure sites he'd been reduced to searching for information on TRIAD.

The site was short on facts and long on messages from fans of the rogue organization. Not as raunchy as the CIA/SAD fan sites, but full of sickening letters from wing-nut supporters of the previous administration's torture policies.

Who and wherever you are, bless you for keeping us safe. Anybody threatening our country deserves to die.

You're the true patriots, not the bozos in the military who don't really even want to be fighting.

They've kicked you out of the CIA, but you'll kick ass soon.

Anybody with information on this fine organization, please contact me.

Hey, Middie, you want to swap?

Middie. Swap what?

More mindless praise. What was it about people that made them glorify outlaws? Yeah, some of the USA's most memorable individuals had been outlaws; in fact, the country—particularly the West—had been defined by them. But the same people who idealized outfits like TRIAD would scream like trapped eagles if anyone ever probed into *their* lives.

Another posting for Middie: *We're waiting.*

And another: *Come on in, Middie.*

Middle of the road? Midshipman? Midtown?

Wait a minute. Mick checked his files. Ryan Middleton's nick-name was Middie.

Swap. Trade wife for information?

Mick checked the date of the postings: the first on Sunday night, the last yesterday evening.

Was TRIAD using this little fan site to contact Middleton? How could they know their messages would reach him?

Easy—Middleton had been an intelligence specialist. If he was on the run and trying to reach Piper, he would monitor every possible source from untraceable places like Internet cafés.

Mick kept reading. More mindless praise. More bad logic.

Then a posting from three hours ago: *Middie, how about a C KRUIZE?*

What the hell?

Sea cruise? Why the eccentric spelling? But then it might be a person's name, a place, an anagram....

Lots of possibilities.

Mick clicked on his and Derek's new search engine, soon to be up and running under the management of Omnivore. Whenever possible, use the very best.

HY RIPINSKY

The chopper had touched down on top of RI's building, but before Hy could get out, an employee came scuttling under the rotors calling out to the pilot. Mr. Morland wanted to know how soon they would return to their destination to the north?

Hy smiled grimly. Craig had observed the organization's need-to-know policy. And a good thing, given what had gone down there earlier.

"Mr. Ripinsky?" the pilot said.

"Go now. I'm riding with you."

The pilot didn't protest; he knew better than to question the boss's judgment. Hy gave the employee a thumbs-up sign as the chopper rose again.

Shar and Craig must've found something that required their quick transport back to the city, he thought. Or else the rifle shots and chopper had attracted unwanted interest in the property. Either way, he was here to see that they got out safely.

"Reconnoiter the property before you attempt to put down," he said to the pilot through their headsets. "And let me have your weapon." All RI pilots were firearms-qualified and had handgun carry permits.

The man handed a .38 back to him without a question.

Moments crawled by as Hy stared moodily down at the changing terrain. His shoulder throbbed dully, but he didn't have a fever or any other symptoms of infection. Still, the wound would slow him down for a while. He'd have to ground himself from flying till it was fully healed.

And McCone? Would she experience a setback from the rigorous activity? She'd been winded and pale when he left, but otherwise seemed okay.

All of this mess had happened because McCone couldn't leave the disappearance of her friend alone, but Hy couldn't condemn her. Quite the opposite. She'd go to extremes for those she cared about, and it was an example a legion of people—himself included—would do well to follow.

He made a couple of calls, again requesting the pilot's permission, then watched as the sea and the retreating fog bank appeared over the pine-blanketed hills. He checked his watch—seventeen after one in the afternoon. Yesterday had flowed seamlessly into today, and today might well do the same into tomorrow. But something had quickened in his blood, and he sensed a resolution coming before too long. Good or bad, he couldn't say.

But a resolution.

The pilot flew low over the Samson property. No cars, no sign of new arrivals.

"Put her down," Hy said.

As the chopper hovered closer and closer to the ground, he saw McCone step out of the trees and wave. She was alone. And smiling—thank God.

But where the hell was Craig?

CRAIG MORLAND

He tapped the steering wheel of Adah's Prius in impotent rage. Tie-up on the fucking Golden Gate Bridge, stalled car in a southbound lane, traffic squeezing around it. Angry drivers, resigned drivers, drivers moving their heads to music, and—of course—the inevitable driver talking away illegally on a cell phone, even though that practice, at least without a hands-free device, had been outlawed for a couple of years now.

In such situations Craig often entertained a fantasy about jumping out of his vehicle and running off on foot to his destination, leaving others to clean up the mess he'd created. After all, hadn't that person who couldn't keep his or her car from stalling created one for him? A Volvo nosed in front of him, and he had a vicious urge to accelerate and smash into it. He calmed himself by thinking of Adah and how she loved the Prius. If she came back and found so much as a scratch on it there'd be hell to pay.

If she came back.

Who was he kidding?

An extra lane branched off right before the toll plaza. He sped into it, and through the booth, his FasTrak registering on the monitor. The pier was his logical destination, but once on Marina Boulevard he was only a few blocks from home.

He needed a few moments of peace. And besides, the cats would be wanting food—they hadn't been fed in a while.

He took a sharp right on Cervantes and another on Beach. And came home to the unexpected.

MICK SAVAGE

C Kruize Control: an Italian disc jockey hosting Nigerian parties and clubs worldwide.
Norman H. Kruise, genealogy.
C. Kruise Reddick: NHL drafts, Twin Cities.
C. K. Videos: ass booty pole dancing.
Kon Centsus Kruize: gambling site, based on an offshore ship.
Kruise Funeral Home, San Antonio, Texas.
Candy Kruize: lots of listings. A real entrepreneur.
Kruise as a baby name: general consensus no.
KruiseforKids: fundraiser for Camp YesICan.

And more, and more...

He sighed and finished the cold dregs of the coffee that Alison had brought that morning. Coffee and croissants for everybody because she thought they were all probably working too hard to bother with breakfast. She had no idea what they were working on, but she'd heard the weariness and tension in his voice when she called his cell that morning. It was a generous thing to do, and Mick appreciated her thoughtfulness, but he'd known her only two days and already she was behaving like a long-term girlfriend—or a wife.

Long-term was great, either way, but there were areas of his life that he didn't open up until he knew and trusted a person, and his work for the agency was one of them. She was moving in too quickly and it made him nervous.

My God, Savage, you've got a beautiful woman interested in you, and you're faulting her for bringing breakfast? Give her a break!

He went back to the C Kruizes, and variations thereof.

Kruise Family History: famed Iowa family.
Kruize Photographic Supply, New Brunswick, New Jersey.
C Cruises: houseboat rentals in the California Delta.
C-More Cruises: tours of Fiji.
Tom Cruise: now, this was getting ridiculous!
Cruises, Okay!: a site for travel agents to advertise.
Kargo Cruises: for those who didn't mind steerage.
Carnival Cruises, Viking Cruises, Galapagos Islands Cruises,
    Cut-Rate Cruises, Norwegian Lines...

A lot of cruise lines. Mick had never been on a cruise. That Galapagos Islands tour might be interesting.

Cruise lines...

He altered his search slightly and began running through the new results.

SHARON McCONE

I was plenty pissed at Hy for coming back on the chopper instead of seeing the doctor as he'd promised, but I tried not to show it. I knew all too well how it felt to be criticized for how I handled my own health care issues, and I didn't want to subject him to similar treatment. Even though he'd been the major critic of mine. Besides, he looked and seemed to be feeling all right. No fever...I had felt his forehead to make sure.

On the way back over the Bay I told him where his Rover was, that somebody would have to fetch it from the secluded place Craig had parked it and that it was safe until arrangements could be made. Then I showed him the keys and tag Craig had found. He examined them, shook his head.

"Could be from any hotel or motel."

"But an older place because of the condition of the tag."

"And the condition of these two keys." He fingered them.

"Somebody may have had the tag for a long time and slipped new keys on the ring."

"Why not take the old keys off and throw them away?"

"Because maybe they still work for some lock."

I was silent for a time, taking the tag from him and running my fingers over its surface. Then I asked, "Any new information come in?"

"If it has, Ted didn't know about it when I talked to him."

"Have you called home? Spoken with Gwen?"

"Yes, on the way back from Marin the first time. She's doing fine. She's one resilient young lady, and Trish and Chelle Curley have been looking in on her."

"When we get back, will you ask somebody from RI to drop me at Richman Labs, and then go see that doctor?"

"McCone, I'm okay."

"Humor me. And keep your promise this time."

CRAIG MORLAND

Rupert Joslyn, Adah's father, was sitting on their couch holding That One, surprising the hell out of Craig when he walked into the apartment.

"Sorry," Rupert said, "I used my key. Thought something might've happened to Adah. Or you."

"Why would you think that?"

"Son, you know Adah's called her mother every Monday night since she moved into her own place at eighteen. Barbara's been beside herself for two nights now, but she didn't want to interfere, in case there was trouble between you two. I fed these critters, by the way."

Craig hung his keys on the rack by the front door, went to his recliner chair, and sat down, head in hands.

"You okay?" Rupert asked.

"No."

"Need a drink?"

"Yes."

"Still into Irish whiskey?"

"Uh-huh. Bottle's in the cabinet—"

"I know where you keep your liquor." Rupert got up, sliding That One to the floor.

Craig raised his head and watched the big, barrel-chested man, white-haired and slightly bowlegged, walk into the kitchen.

How was he going to tell him about Adah? She was the Joslyns' only child and they delighted in her. Had worried about her every day she'd been on the police force, had been thrilled when she'd moved to the admin job at the agency. They loved him like a son, counted on him to take care of her. Well, he'd done one hell of a job, hadn't he?

Rupert returned with two glasses, handed one to Craig. "Now tell me what's wrong."

Craig threw back most of the Irish and then laid the story out for Rupert, omitting some details and trying to keep a positive note.

The old man flinched once, then went back to the kitchen for the bottle of Bushmill's. As he poured, he said slowly, "I think we won't tell Barbara about this."

"Why not?"

"She has a bad heart. We haven't talked about it to you kids, because she doesn't want to worry you. It's not all that life-threatening, but a shock like this..."

"Right. We won't tell her, then."

"So what's being done about the situation?" In spite of the bad news, Rupert had recovered quickly. His eyes were keen and his posture told Craig he'd adopted a battle mode. A former labor organizer for longshoremen, he was as tough as ever.

Craig gave him a capsule report of what had happened in Marin.

"And what're the folks at the agency doing?"

"Pursuing it."

"Meaning you're not up to speed on them."

"I just got back—"

"Hell's afire, man! This is Adah we're talking about."

"You're right. Let's you and I go in for a briefing."

SHARON McCONE

A Richman Labs tech was able to tell me the number on the key tag—112 C—and provided an enhanced image of the design below it, a sunset, as I'd previously guessed. Nothing else to indicate what kind of establishment it came from. That in itself was odd, because the tag was of a vintage—seventies to eighties, he said—when many lodging places had an address printed on their tags to which the key could be returned postpaid if the guest lost it or forgot to turn it in.

No longer, in these days of extreme security precautions.

The newer keys—one to a dead bolt, the other to a heavy-duty padlock—the tech said were commonly available and had probably been cut in the past year. The others were from the same period as the tag. One was to a standard snap lock, the other one didn't show up on any of their references. The tech had put out inquiries as to what kind of lock it might operate.

I called Chelle from the lab and asked her to pick me up and deliver me to the pier. She said she'd have to come in my MG, so it might take a while. It did, and when she pulled to the curb she stalled the engine.

"Look, Chelle," I said when I got in, "you have to learn to operate a stick shift better. You're ruining the MG's gearbox. That ride to the pier to borrow Ted's car the other day was a nightmare."

"I know. Stalling on the Muni tracks wasn't my finest hour."

"We can't keep appropriating Ted's car."

"Um, I hate to say it but . . . even if I could drive a stick well, your car is a piece of crap."

"You're talking about my classic MG!"

"Crap."

"The agency van is an automatic—"

"And it's usually needed for people running surveillances. You've got to buy an inconspicuous, reliable personal car."

"With an automatic transmission."

"Right."

Reliable and inconspicuous: those were the key words. The MG hadn't been either for some time now, despite a new engine and transmission. Just as with Hy's ancient Morgan and the classic Mustang he had replaced it with, it should be put out of its misery or sold to somebody who had the patience, money, and time to keep it restored and running.

But a boring car with an automatic transmission?

I pictured myself driving along the coast highway without the control and satisfaction of downshifting on the curves, upshifting on the straightaways. Driving—like flying—had been an intense source of pleasure and adventure to me; I'd been so looking forward to getting back to it.

But not in some slug of a car.

"I'll think about it," I said. And I would—until next summer when I could drive myself again. In the meantime I'd rent something inexpensive from Enterprise for Chelle.

She must've sensed my thoughts, because she said, "You and that vehicle are gonna be buried together."

The agency hummed with purposeful activity as I climbed to the catwalk. I stopped in at Ted's office for a briefing. Craig had come in with Rupert Joslyn in tow—permissible to brief Adah's father, under the circumstances—and now they were with Patrick, going over the case's status.

"So Craig finally told Adah's parents."

"No. Rupert came to him because they hadn't heard from her."

"How're he and Barbara holding up?"

"He's pitched in. Barbara doesn't know yet." There would be hell to pay when she found out, even if Adah was returned to them safely.

Thelia, Ted added, had gotten a hit on one of Adah's credit cards and gone out to interview the clerk at the convenience store in San Rafael where it had been used.

San Rafael—approximately halfway between Inverness and the city. But could Bob Samson have used a card with an obviously female name on it?

"Did Thelia mention what time the card was used?"

"After two in the morning."

Possibly the woman who had visited Samson? He would have taken Adah's ID from her, maybe left it somewhere in his cabin where the woman had found and pocketed it.

"Anything else?" I asked.

"Beyond the usual calls from your family? As of this minute, I have twelve messages for you—all of them urgent."

I sighed. "*None* of them urgent. Just stack them in my in-box, unless somebody dies—which isn't likely."

"Speaking of your family, Mick is onto something. Steaming. Better go cool him down."

Steaming was the right word for it. He didn't even look up, just waved me to Derek's chair and went on staring at the monitor, clicking again and again.

I said, "I want you to look at something—"

"Not now."

"What are you—?"

"Be quiet!"

"That machine isn't *talking* to you. Can't you listen and talk at the same time?"

"No!"

"All right." There was a time, I thought, when the little shit hadn't dared talk to me like that. Of course, he wasn't a little shit anymore, and if he told me to shut up, there was probably good reason.

Click, click, click...

God, he really was onto something.

A minute, two, three...

A final click and the printer started up.

"So?" I asked.

"Wait a minute."

"In the meantime, can I give you something I need you to work on?"

He held up his hand, then removed the sheet the printer spat out and extended it to me at the same time I extended the enhancement of the key tag that Richman Labs had provided.

They were the same: a sunset. Only at the top of Mick's page there was a logo.

Circle K Cruises, San Francisco.

Circle K was a defunct cruise line that had plied the waters between the city and various Mexican ports from 1980 till 2004, when they'd gone bankrupt. They'd owned four ships, two of which had been sold for scrap and two that had been purchased by a rival company but never been put into service. The *Circle Star* and the *Circle Diamond* were berthed at a mothball fleet in a small private marina on San Pablo Bay, north of the sprawling suburb of Hercules and south of Richmond-Carquinez Bridge.

Circle K Cruises. Piper and Ryan Middleton had won a cruise to Mexico in a supermarket raffle and decided to make it their honeymoon. On Circle K? That would dovetail nicely. It fit with the messages to Middie, wanting to swap.

"Bring up the Quinn file," I told Mick.

There it was—the happy couple had been given their choice of Circle K ships. No mention of which one they'd chosen.

"Find out more about that location, where those out-of-commission ships are berthed," I said.

"Don't need to. I know it pretty well. A biker buddy of mine lives just down the road from there." He drew up a map on the screen. "One way in and one way out of there. Here"—he moved the cursor—"is the road. And here is a little houseboat colony that the residents call World's End. And down at the end of the road is the commercial mothball fleet."

"Pretty deserted out there?"

"Reasonably. World's End is a quirky, rundown little community. A few people who live there are probably hiding out from the law. Others like their privacy and being on the water. They're all eccentric, so they can tolerate each other's weirdnessess. You can't see the mothball fleet from there because a point juts out between them. I doubt anybody ever goes to the end of the road. At least I've never seen anyone."

"I think somebody has. Recently. Can your friend get us out there?"

"I'd say this guy can do just about anything."

ADAH JOSLYN

There were no more screams or gunshots, and the men's voices were silent. Adah listened intently but heard nothing. Finally she went to sit on the quilt.

Okay, what had she heard? An argument, gunshots, and a woman screaming. And the reverberations of the shots had produced an image of the place's shape and size.

She was on a ship. Docked someplace sheltered, which accounted for the creaking, the dank smell, and the slight motions on the water. The drip—a slow leak somewhere? There had to be holding tanks for water on board, because it was available to her in the bathroom. What if they ran out and she had no supply?

She and Craig had taken a cruise in the Caribbean last spring. Princess Lines—the *Golden Princess*. This ship, she sensed, was older and much smaller, and the cabin on a lower deck than theirs had been. And it had been out of commission for a while. Where was it berthed?

Somewhere in the Hunters Point area? A lot of storage marinas there. Somewhere else on the chain of bays and waterways that ran from the Golden Gate to the Sacramento Delta? A lot of territory, much of it sparsely populated.

She pictured the Delta: narrow levee roads, weedy marshes, fertile fields. Suisun Bay: bordered on one side by farmland and on the other by suburban sprawl. Carquinez Strait: spanned by two wide, soaring bridges. San Pablo Bay: an expanse stretching from the poverty-stricken former military town of Vallejo to San Francisco Bay. The Port of Oakland and the South Bay: shores crowded with industry, hotels, homes, and the airport.

No, she wasn't in a marina at Oakland or in the South Bay; if she was she'd've heard traffic sounds, planes taking off and arriving at the area's two major airports. San Francisco Bay was the same—too populated. Somewhere north, then. Tucked away in a place where few people ever came. But not so remote that it didn't have a nearby McDonald's: the food her captor brought her had still been warm.

Well, no point in further speculation. Before the people had arrived, argued, and the shot had been fired, she'd almost gotten the door open. She'd start working on it again, have to chance that they were gone now and get herself the hell out of here.

No matter who or what she found aboard, nothing was worse than this dank, stuffy prison.

CRAIG MORLAND

He drove over the Bay Bridge from the city, hands tensed on the wheel, eyes focused on what the spreading beams of the SUV's headlights revealed to him. Took I-80 to the Hercules exit and passed through outskirts of suburbia that were like outskirts everywhere—Taco Bell, Mickey D's, Burger King, KFC; malls and strip malls. Shar, sitting beside him, was equally tensed, and her mouth twitched frequently. With pain? He remembered what she'd told him about the constant sharp pain that had plagued her in the months since she'd been recovering from her locked-in state:

It's like a vicious animal that has hold of you, gnawing. Sometimes you think it's gone away. But after minutes of relief, it's back with its big sharp teeth.

Was she in that kind of pain now? He glanced at her.

No. Her grimace was one of determination and just plain rage. What he felt.

"There's the road we want," she said. "Turn left."

In the backseat, Mick's phone rang.

"Okay," Mick said after he'd ended the call. "My friend has a boat and he knows that marina. We'll go out there and—"

"Craig and I will go out there," Shar told him. "Not you."

"I can help—"

"An extra person who's not armed is only going to be in the way."

"But the guy who took Adah is dead. There's not going to be anybody there but her."

"Are you forgetting TRIAD? You have no idea how many people they have—or where they've stashed Piper."

Mick fell silent. Feeling impotent, Craig thought. The way he'd felt for so long without the prospect of action. The way Rupert must feel. The old man hadn't liked it when they'd told him he couldn't come along, had shouted that a man had a right to try to save his daughter, that he was tough enough, fit enough to help. It had taken a lot of persuasion to get him to go home and wait for word.

"Turn left here," Mick said.

They'd been paralleling the shoreline and the I-80 freeway. Now the lights on the hills behind them sparkled in the clear sky. The moon was bright and full.

"The road to World's End is coming up in about fifty yards," Mick said. "Long row of mailboxes there."

Craig spotted them, turned again. His headlights picked out an abandoned car and a trailer on blocks, a half-sunken fishing trawler, a dredger listing to one side in the oily black water.

"People *live* here?"

"Quite a few of them."

They passed a newish cabin cruiser, lights aglow. A collapsing shack, and a corrugated metal Quonset hut. A wrecked craft that looked as if it had been through the war in the Pacific. A houseboat with its stern immersed.

"Stop here."

Another houseboat with shingles that were weathered gray; intact, riding high on the water. Smoke came from a stovepipe chimney and light spilled around blinds in the windows. As Craig pulled the SUV to the side of the rutted road, a man emerged onto the sagging dock, shotgun cradled in his arms. His hands tensed on the wheel.

"No worries," Mick said. "It's only my friend Leon. The gun is just in case—he's got a thing about his privacy."

SHARON McCONE

I liked Leon Moskowitz from the moment we stepped inside his houseboat. A giant with shiny clean dark hair pulled back in a neat ponytail, clad in olive-green sweats. Muscular body, gentle manner, clear intuitive gaze. He hugged Mick, called him "little brother" and enveloped all our hands in his own large one.

He laid the shotgun in a rack and said, "So I hear we're going for a boat ride."

I said, "This may be dangerous."

"So Mick told me. I never shied away from danger in my life."

"You're sure?" I asked.

"Yeah."

"This isn't your fight."

"Somebody's in trouble in my territory, it's my fight."

This man would be a definite asset to our search, I thought. Everything about him spelled confidence.

"Okay. Thank you." I motioned at the gun rack. "Better bring that along."

"I got others on the boat. Rifle, and a handgun. You carrying?"

"Yes. Both of us."

"Then we're set to go. You hold down the fort here, little brother, monitor us on the ship-to-shore. If we call for reinforcements, go next door and have Rab come out. I've already briefed him on the situation."

Mick's mouth turned pouty again, but he didn't argue.

Leon led us from the cabin and down the dock to a small but fast-looking power boat tied up at its end. He and I got on board while Craig undid the lines. The boat's engine burbled as we pushed off.

Leon steered us toward the open water. I sat beside him, Craig leaning on the back of my seat. The marina was dead calm, its lights receding behind us. There was a light wind, and the smells of salt water and creosote were strong. Something else in the air, too—raw and unpleasant, perhaps oil seeping from the older craft or from the refineries south at Point Richmond. Craig was keyed up, but I felt surprisingly calm.

Leon said, "Mick filled me in on what you're after, but before I get myself to a place where I might get my ass shot off, I want to know all of it."

After Craig and I finished providing as many of the details as we were willing to divulge, the big man was silent for a moment. Then he said, "You know, it fits. That storage yard, they've got security on it, but not much. And you know which security company? Morell Associates."

"No surprise there," I said. "And I'll bet the operative they assigned to it was Bob Samson."

"Big blond guy? Dresses like a cowboy?"

"Yes."

"That's your man. Any chance he's standing guard out there?"

"Not anymore."

"Anybody else?"

I glanced at Craig. We hadn't told Leon about TRIAD, but given the circumstances he had a right to know about that too.

Craig felt the same. He said, "There're some other people involved. Rogue CIA agents on a mission."

The silence stretched out so long I half expected Leon to turn the boat around and head for home.

"Hell," he finally said, "I've seen combat. Army, Afghanistan.

Paratrooper, airborne cannon fodder. You don't wanna be there, but you put your life on the line anyway. I mean, it's your *country*, you gotta defend it. But those pussy spooks, sneaking around, hiding in their bunkers in DC, taking women hostage—cowards, worse'n politicians. Man, I hate them!"

I said, "So you'll help us, even if we weren't exactly up-front with you?"

"Yeah I will. Whatever it takes, count me in all the way."

The near full moon lay a shimmery path on the water, dancing this way and that, playing tricks with my eyes. We encountered some higher waves once in the open bay between the two coves, but the surface of the mothball marina lay motionless ahead of us, the moonpath straight and flat. Security lights threw out a dull orange glow. The night had grown icy, and I burrowed into my down jacket. Craig was shivering—whether from cold or nervous tension, I couldn't tell. Only Leon seemed unaffected by the temperature.

He throttled back at the entrance to the marina and gestured to the right and left. "*Circle Star, Circle Diamond.*" He handed me a pair of binoculars.

I scanned the area. No signs of activity, no other small craft tied up there. Both old cruise ships were dark, as were the others nearby.

Of course, what the dark conceals...

I handed the glasses to Craig. After a moment I heard his sharp intake of breath. Not because he'd seen something—because he was imagining Adah somewhere inside one of those hulks, helpless and afraid.

"Which d'you want to tackle first?" Leon asked. "*Star* or *Diamond*?"

"Your call, Craig."

His reply was swift and firm: "*Diamond.*"

"Why?" I asked.

"For luck. Because if we get Adah out of this, I'm going to marry her."

ADAH JOSLYN

The dead bolt finally gave, and she sank back on her heels, breathing deeply. She hadn't realized how finely her senses had been honed till now. The muscles of her arms quivered, her fingers and back ached, and she felt the beginning of a cramp in her right calf. Quickly she got to her feet and put her whole weight on the leg; the cramp eased.

For a moment she stood staring at the door.

Open it and you're out of here and into God-knows-what.

Anything's better than this place.

She patted her pocket for the bolt. Grabbed and twined the garrote in her fingers. Small weapons against unknown danger—but at least they gave her courage.

She turned the knob and inched the door open.

Fresh air filled her nostrils. Not what she normally would've considered fresh, and still dank, but like pure oxygen compared to the stink of the cabin. Cooler, too—it felt good on her skin for a moment. Then she shivered. Silence enveloped the vessel; the dripping sound was faint behind her. She couldn't see much. The light from the bathroom didn't reach but a couple feet beyond the door.

What it revealed were water-stained walls, capped wires protruding from them where fixtures had been removed. Acoustic tiles that had fallen from the ceiling. Threadbare brown carpet.

Pure black to her right—how often did you encounter that? Usually there were shades of gray, darker objects layered upon the lighter ones. But this—it was eerie. Like waking up one day and finding you were totally blind. To the left, far down the corridor, a pale shaft of light shone from above.

She went that way.

CRAIG MORLAND

It was a snap decision to search the *Diamond* first, and now he wasn't sure it was right. The ship wasn't big by today's cruise ship standards, but going through it would take hours, and after all, there were only three of them. Meantime Adah might be imprisoned on the *Star*. But what else could they do? Flip a coin?

The devil of this was the not knowing. Adah leaving him, Adah diagnosed with a serious illness, even Adah being killed in a car accident—at least he would *know*. But not knowing, waiting through days, weeks, months...

It was the worst thing he could imagine.

Leon Moskowitz said, "Craig? You okay, man?"

Pretend it isn't Adah out there. Pretend you're still with the Bureau and you've got a job to do.

He fingered his service revolver tucked into the waistband of his jeans, thought of all the times he'd been grateful not to have to use it. Thought of all the times it had saved his life.

He'd use it tonight, in an instant.

"Yeah, I'm all right," he said. "Let's go for the *Diamond*."

ADAH JOSLYN

She felt her way along the dark corridor, hands snagging on rough wallboard, feet catching on tears in the carpet. The air had grown thick with a familiar odor that she wished she could ignore. Someone dead somewhere in here. One of the men or the woman she'd heard quarreling, likely.

The faint light from above had to be coming down a stairway to an upper deck. The death smell was more intense as she advanced—

She tripped. Went down hard, grazing her chin on the carpet. Pain zigzagged through her body and the air whooshed out of her lungs. When she could breathe again and her nerve endings had stopped screaming, she realized she was lying on a body.

A dead body.

Jesus!

Her already queasy stomach roiled. She pushed back, reared up, grabbed something protruding from the wall for balance. To her touch it felt like a support for one of the handrails that customarily line a ship's corridors. It sliced into her hand and drew blood.

She told herself it was no worse than being at a homicide scene. She'd visited hundreds of those. But she had never fallen on a victim. Never touched one without latex gloves.

She felt her hand. Not a big gash, but potentially dangerous in a place like this. When was her last tetanus shot? She couldn't remember.

Finally she hunkered down beside the body. Male or female? Male: he had a thick beard. Thick hair too. About six feet tall, she estimated, of normal weight for a man of his height. Down jacket, jeans, running shoes. His flesh was cool and pliant—rigor hadn't set in yet.

She read his face with her fingers. Bushy brows, high forehead, straight nose. Skin smooth, except for a scar on his right cheek.

Her captor?

No, that man had been stockier. And she had a subjective sense of him that would be hard to explain to someone who hadn't gone through the experience. This was someone else entirely.

She searched his clothing, hoping to find identification or a weapon. There was a wallet, and she pocketed it. No gun. If he'd come aboard armed, the shooter had taken it. Too bad; she could have used it.

She thought back to the argument and shots she'd heard. How long ago had that been? Hours, it seemed, but her sense of time was so skewed. The condition of the body told her it couldn't have been too long.

Was this man's killer still aboard? Wouldn't he have wanted to put as much distance between himself and this ship as possible? Maybe, maybe not. He could be waiting and watching above.

Chance she'd have to take.

Adah stepped over the body, felt her way down the corridor toward the pale shaft of light.

THURSDAY, FEBRUARY 12

SHARON McCONE

A few minutes after midnight.

Leon said, "Better have your weapons ready. Doesn't look like anybody's on board the *Diamond*, but if somebody was, he wouldn't be showing light. I'll keep her at low throttle and maneuver with the running lights off."

I glanced at Craig; he was removing his revolver from his waistband, chin set, dead calm except for a tic beside his left eye. For a moment there he'd looked uncertain, vulnerable, but now he was back in his fed mode—a shield against what we might or might not find.

My .357 felt solid and comforting in my hand. I'm good with firearms and have never hesitated to use them when necessary, but that doesn't mean I'm infatuated with them. They're a tool of the trade, manufactured only for one reason—and I've never let anybody tell me otherwise.

Leon's eyes swept the marina—back and forth, glinting in the moonlight. The power on the boat was so low it barely made a murmur. We glided smoothly over the flat water, the *Diamond* riding low before us.

It was indeed a derelict ship, listing against the dock, coated in rust, deck railings mostly missing. The way it sat in the water told me that at least the lower deck—the hold and engine room—was flooded. There were no lifeboats or signal tower, and the bridge looked to be partially collapsed.

I fingered the key tag in my pocket: C deck. Crew's quarters on a ship this size, and if I remembered rightly from my one and only cruise, well above the waterline the *Diamond* had sunk to. Small cabins with no portholes, few amenities. And now in ruin. I tried to imagine being imprisoned in such a place. Couldn't.

Either this or the *Star* had to be the right ship. If we'd correctly interpreted the presence of the keys in Adah's car and the messages for "Middie" on the TRIAD site. Wherever she was, Adah was still alive. I refused to think otherwise.

And what about Piper? She'd somehow gotten lost in the other urgencies of our investigation, was mentioned only as the cause of Adah's disappearance.

I touched the opal pendant she'd given me. I hadn't taken it off since her disappearance. Call it superstition, call it faith, call it hoping for just plain dumb luck. It would remain around my neck until I knew what had happened to her.

Leon whispered, "I'm gonna cut the power off now. There're oars in that rear storage compartment. We can row her up to the dock."

Craig was looking through the binoculars. "Still no lights or any other signs of habitation. She's buttoned up tight. But there's what looks like a long ladder lying on the dock beside her."

I said. "So somebody's been aboard recently?"

"Would seem so. The ladder is an extension type; given how low that ship has sunk, it'd reach to the passenger deck."

"I'll bet it was brought here by Bob Samson. Convenient of him to leave it for us."

"Well, he meant to come back." Craig's voice was clipped. Expecting the worst, steeling himself.

My cell phone vibrated. Irritated, I pulled it out to check who was calling. Not a call—a text message from the tech at Richman Labs. I read it, then whispered to the others, "The odd key on that ring was of a type used to lower and raise gangplanks on small ships. But why did Samson quit using it?"

Leon shrugged. "That'd be the first mechanism to stop working on a rusted-out tub like this."

In any case, now we knew why two of the four keys were old and salt corroded. The new one for the padlock—probably on the marina's gate—and the dead bolt had been installed by Bob Samson.

Craig had gotten out the oars from a storage compartment. The power was off. I moved to take one of them, but Leon motioned me aside. "You watch, make sure we don't slam into that dock."

Closer, closer, and then he told Craig to stop paddling and swung the boat around to port side. It stopped inches from a piling. Craig jumped out and started securing it. Leon followed. I stepped onto the rickety planks and went for the ladder. It was newish looking and not very heavy, but I was grateful when both men took over most of the burden. One thing I'd learned over the past few days was to ask for help when I needed it.

I dropped down on the ship's deck behind Craig and waited till Leon had followed. The moon was on the wane, but it still illuminated our surroundings. The deck—planks buckled, rotted, and missing—stretched to either side of us. Ahead was a corroded wall and a door with a porthole in it. There had been large picture windows aft, but all that remained was their frames.

Cold here, and it must be colder inside. Adah hated the cold; Craig always complained about their heating bills.

Leon nudged me. "We going in there?"

"Yes. I'm not sure where, though."

Craig moved into a crouch on the other side of me. "Those windows aft—they're all broken out, easy entry."

"Let's do that."

We moved single file. The deck creaked with every one of our steps. If Verke or his TRIAD cohorts were here, they'd hear us and prepare a grand reception.

A few feet from the first broken window I held up my hand to stop the others. I could see through it to the aft deck and a drained and fractured swimming pool. There were shards of glass—sharp and deadly—sticking out of the window frame. Craig and I eased them loose, set them aside. Then we boosted ourselves over the sill.

Silence, heavy and empty-feeling.

Safe to use a low-beamed flashlight now. Craig took his out of his pocket.

The space had been stripped, but I could tell that once there had been a long bar with a mirror backing it. I imagined the honeymooners—Piper and Ryan—sitting on stools, holding hands and sipping exotic drinks that only people on cruises or holiday in the tropics order. Silly love talk and bright future plans and thinking it would go on forever. Lounging by the pool, faces turned up to the sun, and with not a suspicion of how it would end.

Craig's light pointed to the exit. And we went on.

We moved through empty spaces, echoing and eerie in the flash's beam. Craig held up his hand, motioned at narrow corridors to either side of the ship. I pointed to myself and then to the starboard side, indicated that he and Leon should go to port. We parted, and I found myself moving along what seemed to be a dark tunnel with no end in sight. Stepping carefully, feeling the walls. I had my own light, but its beam was pencil thin and dim. I had to train it on the floor to avoid gaps in the decking.

To my right was a doorway. I paused, shone the light through it. A large room containing nothing but a huge pot rack on one wall, curved hooks like the upturned claws of a dead animal. Part of the ship's galley.

I turned the flash away and kept going.

ADAH JOSLYN

H er legs felt leaden as she inched along the corridor toward the pale shaft of light. For all she knew there were other bodies in here; the death smell was still sharp in the cold air. She measured her progress in the spaces between handrail supports. When she finally reached a stairway leading up into the light, she paused to listen.

Silence.

The stairway led onto another corridor, this one with once deep-piled blue carpet worn thin by time and red flocked wallpaper that was coming down in great swathes. A single yellowish bulb burned there. No reason for a security light here—it had to've been left on by her captor.

She moved along the corridor looking through the open doors. Cabins, but unlike the one where she'd been confined, these had portholes. She must've been in the crew's quarters. Another stairway, another corridor. More cabins, larger. She hurried past, found a stairwell midway down, and climbed to a large room that ran the width of the ship. Stood still and tried to get a sense of the place.

Main salon, probably, where the concierge and business offices were. Off it would extend spaces once occupied by the dining hall, bar, small shops, maybe a movie theater or a nightclub. There might've been a pool on the afterdeck. Shuffleboard courts.

She sensed that only the Spartan remainders of the ship's

appointments existed now. The vessel howled with emptiness; all items with resale value must've been stripped years ago.

Adah turned to her left. There was a round opening showing grayish light—the door to the deck and freedom? She started toward it, but her knee banged into something and she threw her hands out to keep from falling forward.

What the hell was this? She felt a smooth, cool surface. Round bowl-shaped body. And a shaft extending upward...

A fountain. They'd had a goddamn fountain in the salon. Probably too much of a job to remove it. As she gripped the shaft, a chunk pulled away in her hand. Not marble, but some composition material simulated to feel and look like it. She stuffed it into her pocket—evidence she'd been here.

Another piece cracked off the fountain and made a noise as it fell into the bowl. Adah started.

And someone else gasped.

Immediately Adah went into a fighting stance. "Who's there?"

Silence.

"Where are you?"

More silence.

"Look, I am fucking sick of this game! Who the hell *are* you?"

"Who are *you*?" It was a woman's voice, low and weak. Eva? Had she come back to finish the job she'd started in the stairwell on Tenth Avenue?

"You know the answer to that! You've had me locked up here ever since—"

"No. No, I've been locked up too."

Adah felt an odd tingling at the nape of her neck. Not Eva—another prisoner. "Piper? Piper Quinn?"

"Yes."

Well, thank God. "I'm Adah Joslyn, operations director of McCone Investigations."

Sounds as the woman crawled across the floor, gripped Adah around the knees, and began crying.

Adah put her hand on the woman's head, felt long matted hair. "It's okay," she said. "It's gonna be all right now. Come on, get up. We're leaving this place."

"No! They'll kill me—"

"Nobody's here but us."

"J.T. and Ryan were here. J.T. shot Ryan. I think he killed him. I don't know, though. I ran."

The shots she'd heard. But now was not the time to sort it all out.

"Come on," she said, trying to ease Piper to her feet.

But before she could manage that, new sounds caught Adah's attention: somebody moving around on the deck. She crouched behind the fountain's bowl, pulled Piper down too. And listened.

The footsteps had gone toward the rear of the ship. Adah stopped holding her breath; they had time. Beside her, Piper tugged on her arm. "I know a place we can hide. Where I've been for hours."

Adah followed her. By the far inside wall, where the main desk had been, Piper stopped and dropped down. Adah followed.

The hiding place was a hole where the floorboards had been ripped up. Piper lowered herself, then reached for Adah's hand. The space was small and smelled of dry rot; there were probably the remains of asbestos insulation lurking in there, and Adah wished she had a face mask. She and Piper were crammed in there, shoulder to shoulder.

From aft the stealthy footsteps came on.

"They're on board," she whispered.

In the darkness she felt Piper nod. "What're we going to do?"

"Stay quiet and still. They'll search and be gone. They won't find us."

Yeah, sure.

She listened as the footsteps came closer. Three people—one large, one medium, one smaller. None of them spoke.

Piper was breathing hard now, and Adah was afraid she'd hyperventilate. She linked her arm with hers, held her tight. After a moment Piper's respiration slowed.

The people had entered the main salon now, only yards from this hiding place. Overhead Adah saw light sweeping around. A whisper. Another. She strained to hear.

"C deck?"

"...what's on the key..."

"Got to find her."

She knew that whisper. Had heard it a thousand times. Knew it better than her own. Her pulse rate leaped.

"Craig!"

Piper jerked and clutched her arm. Adah could feel her frantically shaking her head.

"Adah? Oh, God, where are you?"

She freed herself from Piper's grip and poked her head up. Momentarily a flashlight's beam blinded her. Craig called her name again.

"Down here," she called. "Piper's with me. We're both okay."

Running footsteps now and then Craig reached down to her, pulled her up, and they held each other, as if trying to fuse their bodies into one.

SHARON McCONE

Poor Adah. She didn't get any of the things—shower, wine, steak—that she told me she'd fantasized about while locked up—and she certainly didn't get laid. Instead Mick had the paramedics standing by at World's End; they checked her and Piper over and transported them to John Muir Medical Center in nearby Walnut Creek. There they were cleaned up, hydrated, and put to bed. Tomorrow they'd be eating haute cuisine à la hospital. And probably be plenty pissed off.

Adah and Piper had related what had happened to them aboard the derelict ship in Leon's boat on the way back. It was pretty much as we'd theorized.

"Ryan...my husband." Piper paused, pressing her hand to her closed eyes. "He was killed in Iraq, but then he showed up on the ship this morning."

"Looking for you?"

"Yeah. I was the bait."

"Verke is the one who took you?"

"He and a woman named Melinda Knowles...She came to my apartment, said she was an old friend of my mother's." Piper's breath caught, and she coughed, then continued, slurring her words slightly. "She must've...drugged me. I think at one point you were there, but I can't say for sure."

"I was. You were out of it."

"Not as...out of it as I feel now." She shook her head. "It's a... blur."

"She was the same woman who drugged me," Adah said. "Only the man upstairs called her Eva."

I said, "Both were probably aliases. These covert operatives assume so many different identities, it's a wonder they can keep them straight. You don't have to worry about her anymore—she's dead. I think it wasn't in their plans to take anyone other than Piper, but Eva overreacted to Verke's news that an investigator was in the building. Drugging you was a bad mistake, and organizations like TRIAD don't put up with people who make mistakes."

"So Verke killed her in the building?"

"Yes. There was a bullet hole in the second-floor apartment."

"And then he transported her to his ex-wife's house? That doesn't make sense."

"It was a place he had access to, where he could hide the body till it was more convenient to get rid of it. Admittedly, not great thinking, but he probably knew from when he took the van that the ex and her boyfriend were gone and assumed Gwen was with them. He didn't count on her finding and opening the tarp. Or me showing up right after."

I turned to Piper. "What did Verke want from Ryan?"

"A microchip he'd smuggled out of Iraq. But he didn't have it... said it must've been shipped to me along with his other stuff. I told Verke I'd given it all away. He wanted to know to who, but I wouldn't tell." Her words were coming slowly now. She was slipping away from us.

"He got angry...called me names...hit me. A struggle and he shot Ryan. I ran and hid.... Couldn't involve the people at the hospice thrift shop or..." She dozed off, chin dipping toward her breastbone.

J. T. Verke, ex–CIA op, currently working for TRIAD, was on the loose, and I was sure he wouldn't stop looking for the chip. He was a dangerous man who hadn't gotten what he wanted. He'd try again sooner or later.

Hy met us at John Muir, where he posted operatives from RI outside the doors of both Piper's and Adah's rooms. Some influence must have been brought to bear, because the police were not summoned. Hy told me later he'd spun a yarn about two friends out for a boat ride on San Pablo Bay capsizing and getting marooned, and Leon backed him up. I wouldn't have believed it for a moment.

"What about Middleton's body?" I asked. "We can't just leave it there."

Hy's smile was grim. "Why not? He's already dead and buried in Colma."

One man left as coyote fodder in Marin. Another consigned to rot in a derelict ship that eventually would sink into the oily waters of that deserted marina. I shook my head, wished I could close my mind against the knowledge. And what about the family of the man buried in Middleton's grave? Didn't they deserve some consideration?

When I voiced my objection, Hy said, "Adah took a wallet off Middleton's body. The guy who died was Specialist Jay Winters. I'll ask a contact with the military to phone the next of kin and tell them where he's buried."

It still didn't feel right, to abandon a human being's remains to the elements.

But that was probably what Middleton would have done to Adah and Piper.

Not an excuse, but a good reason.

We had to think about further security for Piper until Verke was apprehended, perhaps at RI's safe house near Balboa and Twenty-eighth Avenue. A shabby old apartment house masking high-tech security measures and luxury accommodations for clients in fear for their safety. I'd taken shelter there myself a time or two.

Most of all I was concerned for Piper's emotional state: after she'd been admitted and was in her room, she asked for me and tried to talk, but broke down in tears, spoke incoherently, and had to be sedated. I'd withheld the information she had no home to go back to, no possessions. I was afraid it would break her.

By the time Mick and I returned to the city, it was midmorning. Craig had remained at the hospital, but would be on the phone scheduling a meeting with the regional director of the FBI. Time to come clean and ask their help in locating Verke; with Craig paving the way, he claimed, no proceedings would be brought against the agency. After all, we'd done the majority of their work for them.

From the car I'd called my house to see if Gwen Verke was okay. No answer. I called Chelle's cell: voice mail. Called her home and got Trish.

"No worries," she said. "She and Chelle are out shopping."

"How come?"

"Gwen's got no clothes with her except for what she had on the other night, and she doesn't want to go back to the house in Cupertino."

"But she had only ten dollars. Where's the money for this expedition coming from?"

"I let them take my credit card."

"I'll pay you back—it's on the agency."

"Thanks. You know, Gwen's a nice girl. We could use another one of those around here."

"Then you'll have to protect her." I explained about her father.

"Good God!" Trish said. "Does she know what her father is?"

"I don't think so. They haven't been in touch in quite a while."

"Should I tell her?"

My inclination was to say no, but Gwen needed to be aware she was in danger. "Yes. But first, do this: take her to the RI safe house on Twenty-eighth Avenue. Here's the address."

I waited till she wrote it down. "It's a comfortable place. You'll enjoy it. I'll call security there and alert them that you'll be arriving. Do you mind—just for a couple of days?"

"My husband and child will be perfectly okay without me. I'll consider it a vacation."

By late afternoon the FBI was searching for Verke. Craig told me he'd had to call in many a favor to keep the agency out of trouble. Adah was doing fine and clamoring to go home; she'd sent him out for a steak and said she'd never go near a Mickey D's again.

Piper was another case: they'd transferred her to the psychiatric unit for observation. She'd emerged from the sedation agitated and incoherent; the only thing clear to anyone was that she wanted—no, needed—to talk with me. But when I phoned the charge nurse on the unit, he said that she couldn't have visitors for at least twenty-four hours.

I caught up on some paperwork, talked with Thelia about the upcoming Andersen appeal. Got up to speed with Ted, and looked over Patrick's flow charts. Hy was at home, nursing his wounded shoulder; I'd promised to bring him barbecue takeout—protein, he claimed, was what he needed.

Gradually the pier grew quiet. Patrick left to take his boys to a basketball game. Mick's new woman friend picked him up and they went off in the night to . . . whatever. Thelia said she was going to go home and sleep round the clock. Derek had called to say he'd be back tomorrow and was sorry he hadn't been here to help out. Julia was due in on Monday. Ted and Kendra were inventorying supplies and going over paperwork in their offices: working late, because tomorrow they were respectively taking a long weekend.

And I was exhausted.

Six, even four, months ago I would have never dreamed I could survive days like these last few. Then I'd dreamed only of coming back to some approximation of my former self. But early Wednesday morning, Hy had put it together for me:

"You're all the way back, aren't you?"

"Ripinsky, it feels as if I've never been away."

Yes and no: I'd still have to monitor my health, try to live sensibly. I'd always have the memory of those dark, locked-in days and the fear of never being normal again that had gripped me. But maybe I'd become the new, improved McCone. Imagine that!

Down on the pier's floor a car horn beeped—the squeaky, wimpy horn of a boring, sensible rental car. I gathered my things and went down there; Chelle had arrived to drive me home.

McCONE INVESTIGATIONS

Adah Joslyn

She stirred, came awake, lay listening to the late-night hospital routine. Rustling of garments, rubber-soled shoes squeaking on the floor, hushed voices soothing the occasional complaint of a fellow patient. Craig slept in the chair next to her bed, his mouth open, snoring lightly.

Tomorrow she would go home. Tomorrow life would resume its usual rhythms.

Or would it? Why did she feel there was something about the case she'd forgotten or overlooked?

Ted Smalley

He watched Kendra leave the office, having turned down his offer of a ride. Heading for the apartment she shared with two other women near the Panhandle of Golden Gate Park? Or meeting friends, perhaps a lover? He didn't know much about Kendra; he hadn't gotten her to open up. Strange, because he usually knew people's life stories within hours of meeting them. Another case for the armchair detective.

If only he were completely convinced this current case was closed....

Mick Savage

He sat on the sofa with Alison, wineglass in hand, wearing the new maroon bathrobe she'd bought him. Rain pelted the windows and through the drops the city lights were fractured. Alison held his hand.

They'd really clicked in bed, but Mick still had the sensation the relationship was going too fast. It was a pleasurable feeling, unfamiliar to him, and a little scary.

Maybe, though, it was in the Savage blood: his father had been with his mother since the night he spotted her from the bandstand where his group was playing a dance at her high school. And when Ricky had come together with Rae, it was an explosive spur-of-the-moment high-profile romance. Dad's first marriage had lasted fifteen years and produced six kids. His marriage to Rae would probably last forever.

So why not go for it with Alison?

She squeezed his hand. He squeezed back, but his mind had already started to wander to less pleasant thoughts.

J. T. Verke was still out there. This case was in no way finished.

Craig Morland

He jerked in his sleep and opened his eyes. The first thing he saw was Adah. The soft curves of her body under the hospital blanket, her bedraggled cornrows, her shining eyes...

Watching him. Awake in the darkness.

Craig got up from the chair and sat on the bed, held her hand. She pulled him down beside her. Laid her head against his chest and relaxed, but he knew she wasn't sleeping. That she was worrying about the same missing pieces of the investigation that were bothering him.

Hy Ripinsky

His shoulder pained him, so he got up and took one of the sedatives the doc had given him. Strong—it would knock him out for a good eight hours. Upstairs he heard McCone moving about in the kitchen, getting a glass of wine or a snack, he guessed.

She'd come back to him, to all of them, and he'd never let her slip away again. Life would be good. They'd travel to Touchstone and the ranch. Soon she'd be able to ride King again. And fly. And drive. Before she'd been shot, they'd talked about vacation possibilities: New Zealand, Greece, Istanbul. Now they could really plan....

The sedative was carrying him off when he wondered if she'd manned the house's security system. Of course she had, and would continue to until the threat of J. T. Verke had been neutralized.

SHARON McCONE

Hy was restless—a dull ache in his shoulder, he said, but more likely from consuming an unseemly amount of barbecue—so I let him have the bed and curled up fully dressed on the sitting room couch in front of the fireplace. It was raining hard, and after a few minutes I adjusted the damper, then went to the kitchen for some wine. I was in that state of exhaustion where your mind refuses to shut down, keeps jumping around and denying you sleep.

I sat back down on the couch, stared into the flames.

Adah and Piper were safe, J. T. Verke would soon be in FBI custody, and life would return to what passed for normal.

I touched Piper's pendant. I'd meant to show it to her, explain how it had become a talisman, but that didn't seem right at the time; she'd been so disoriented that I wasn't sure it would compute.

The stone felt smooth and warm, like its fiery colors. I'd fingered it so often this past week, it was a wonder I hadn't worn it thin. But it was thick, thicker than other opals I'd seen. I took the pendant off and examined it. The stone was set in gold, its backing flat, scratched on one edge.

Something flickered in my memory: "It was a present from an old love," Piper had said when she gave it to me. "He bought it intending to win me back, but he wasn't the man I thought he was. Not possible now."

At the time I'd thought she was speaking of a boyfriend, not a husband, but suppose it was Ryan Middleton who bought her the necklace? Wanting to reconcile after the divorce papers were served on him?

Or for another reason? Of course! He left the microchip in his personal effects, faked his own death, and somehow got back into this country with the intention of retrieving it from Piper. But he didn't want to reveal himself to his wife, and TRIAD wanted the chip too.

Why had Verke and cohorts gone to the extremes of taking Piper and wiping out all evidence of her existence? Why not continue holding her in her apartment, rather than the derelict ship? To get Middleton into a situation where they had absolute control, of course. And once they had the chip, they would kill both him and Piper. After all, he was officially dead, and they'd erased her existence.

Piper had told me she'd given away her husband's things. They were mostly junk. But she'd probably kept the pendant because it was pretty, had given it to me because I'd admired it.

I forced a fingernail into the space where its back was scratched. The nail tore but the pressure forced the back off.

Inside was the chip. Similar to but smaller than a chip from a digital camera.

Ironic: I'd been openly wearing what everybody had been looking for all along.

Evidence. Against yet another corrupt defense contractor? TRIAD? Something damning that went straight to the top echelons of US intelligence agencies?

This was a dangerous thing to have in my possession.

I removed the chip from the pendant and took it to the upstairs bathroom. Locked it in the old US Navy ammo box that was bolted to the floor in the linen closet, where it joined my old .38 and my grandmother's garnet earrings. Then I returned to the sitting room.

Piper hadn't told Verke to whom she'd given Middleton's possessions. She said she hadn't wanted to involve the people at the hospice thrift store, but she nodded off before she could finish the sentence. I could hear her voice adding, *Or you.*

Verke by now had figured out she was protecting the recipient of the pendant; odds were, he would guess the gift had been to a friend. But was there a way for him to find out who that friend was?

Yes. Adah had given Verke her card when she talked with him in the second-floor unit on Tenth Avenue. From the card it was a short step to me. Former CIA ops could find out pretty much everything about people they were interested in. Besides, Piper had no real friends other than me. Melinda Knowles had known that and probably passed on my own card to Verke. By now J. T. Verke would know a thousand other details that would make me his next target. Right now he and his cohorts could be watching this house or the pier. Watching the homes of my operatives. Yes, we were all maxed up on security, but that wouldn't stop them for long. I needed to make the first strike.

I went downstairs to wake Hy.

He lay on his back breathing shallowly and didn't respond to my touch. I shook him but he didn't even moan. Must have taken one of those sedatives. No hope for backup from him.

Upstairs again, I called Chelle and asked her if I could stop by for a few minutes.

"That's okay," she said, "I'm up. Working out the cost estimate for this rehab."

Next I called the third-floor apartment at the RI safe house. A reluctant Trish woke Gwen. She came on the phone, her voice heavy with sleep.

"I won't keep you up long," I told her, "but I need to ask you some questions. When was the last time you saw your father?"

"Um...He stopped by the house a few times after the divorce. But he hasn't been there for maybe a year and a half."

"Where was he living then?"

"Washington, DC, I think."

"You have any idea where he stayed when he was here? A hotel? Motel?"

"No. I think it was a place that belonged to a friend of his."

"You know the friend's name, or where the place is?"

"I don't know the guy's name. But once...Dad picked me up and brought me to the city for lunch at Cliff House and a walk on Ocean Beach. On the way he stopped at a building on La Playa, a couple of blocks from the zoo, and left me in the car while he went in to get a heavier jacket."

La Playa: the residential street that paralleled the Great Highway and the sea.

"You remember what block it was?"

"No, but I remember the building. It was one of those weird places that they're always building near the water—all angles and porthole windows. Painted a pukey yellow."

"Did it look like a multiple-unit building?"

"No. It was really small and narrow. But ugl*eee.*"

Leave it to TRIAD to house their agents in a distinctive structure. Invincible, they thought they were. Well, arrogance is what finally takes them down every time.

The rain had stopped when I slipped out the glass door from the bedroom to the backyard, across the slick grass, and through the fence that connected my property with the Curleys'. Chelle's face peered out the kitchen window, startled.

"Somebody might be watching my house," I said. "I'm going to call a taxi to come to this address."

"I can drive you; they won't recognize the rental car."

"I'm not so sure of that. You picked me up at the pier."

"Shar, there were a dozen vehicles going in and out. And the car is not exactly distinctive."

"I still don't think it's a good idea."

"You're worrying about me again."

"With good reason. This is not some ordinary loser skipping out on his child support payments that I'm after."

"You think I don't know that after what's been going on the past few days? This is the guy who took Adah and Piper, right? Gwen's father?"

"Yes. He's dangerous. Ex-CIA gone rogue."

"And if he's watching your house, where're you going?"

"The place where he's hiding out."

"If you know where that is, why don't you just call the feds and tell them, let them arrest him?"

"I need evidence he's there in order for them to get a warrant."

Chelle shook her head. "So you're going there in a taxi, without backup."

Now that she'd put it into words, the idea did seem foolish and dangerous. But I didn't have anyone I could call on for backup: Hy was stone-cold asleep. Julia was thousands of miles away in Hawaii. Mick wouldn't be any help, and his dad would kill me if I put him in jeopardy. Craig was in Walnut Creek with Adah. None of the other operatives were trained for such a situation. Who did I know that was both bold and good with firearms?

"I've got just the person," I said.

Chelle dropped me at Rae and Ricky's and then went home. Ricky was in LA, and that was a relief; he'd've wanted to go along to protect us, but would've been as ineffectual as his son in this kind of situation.

I outlined the case to Rae. She was shocked and angry that I hadn't called her in sooner to help. "You know, I'm part of the team when it needs me. And Adah's my friend."

"Well, I need you now."

"Then let's go."

On the short drive in her little BMW from her house in Sea Cliff to the beach neighborhood, we talked strategy.

"First we need to identify the house," I said. "Then we have to figure out if Verke's there. He may be doing surveillance at the pier or my house, but maybe not. He's got associates to take care of that."

"And if we do find out he's there, we call the fed in charge of the case."

I didn't reply.

"Shar? I don't like this."

"Don't like what?"

"You wanting to go up against this guy yourself."

"I just want to get him out in the open. See him."

"How're you going to do that?"

"Give him something he wants." I touched the pendant, which I'd put on again before leaving my house.

"Sure, you're going to ring his doorbell and hand it to him. And then what—overpower him? I don't think so. Shoot him? No way that's justifiable."

"You want to back out? I can manage without you."

"Don't go getting all defensive on me."

"Sorry."

"Apology accepted. I'll help, but I want you to promise me one thing."

Oh, hell! Rae and her promises. "What?"

"That as soon as we spot the house and determine Verke's home, you call the feds."

"After I get him out of there."

"No. I won't stop the car till you promise me."

Stubborn as a pit bull.

We turned onto La Playa. I scanned the first block: parked cars, mostly beaded with moisture from the recent rain, their windshields smeary with salt cake; muted lights in some of the windows; no moving vehicles or pedestrians. The houses here were only on the east side; the west side between it and the highway choked with dune grass and sea grape. The dwellings in the next two blocks were mixed: luxurious-looking stuccos with balconies overlooking the sea; apartments, one unit stacked atop another; small cottages, some little more than shacks; a fair number of what Gwen had called "those weird places that they're always building near the water."

"You'd think pukey yellow would stand out," I muttered.

"It does." Rae slowed and pointed to the house. We drifted by. There were lights in the front windows and a dark van in the driveway.

"Now," she added, "call the FBI."

She was going to hold me to it. And I knew I'd be a fool not to. As she drove around the block, I dialed the cellular number on one of the cards Special Agent James Baron had given Craig to pass on to us. Got voice mail.

"Jesus," I said. "Aren't the feds supposed to be available twenty-four-seven? Everybody at McCone Investigations is." And then I realized I'd spoken into the phone, and the agent had just come onto the line.

"Sorry," I said. "This is—"

"Sharon McCone. I have caller ID."

"Agent Baron..." I explained the situation.

"Where are you now?"

"Driving around the block where the suspect in the Piper Quinn abduction's house is situated."

"The address, please."

I gave it.

"What kind of vehicle, color, and license plate number?"

"His or mine?"

"Yours, please."

"Black BMW Z4, convertible, license...?"

I looked at Rae. She supplied it.

"Ms. McCone," Baron said, "I know you're accustomed to handling things...your own way. One can't live in San Francisco and not have heard of you. But this time it's going to be done the Bureau's way. Is that clear?"

"Yes."

"I've brought up a map of the site on my computer. Drive past the house again and make a right on Taraval. I know it's a congested area, so double-park or pull in where you can. Our people will be there in ten minutes." I closed the phone and looked at Rae. "Well, for once I've bent to your will."

"A good thing too."

We rode silently, tension building in the little car. We were both in full watchful mode, monitoring the street around us. Still no traffic here, but a few cars hummed by on the Great Highway and I could hear the restless shifting of the surf.

Rae turned on Taraval, where the streetcar line stopped and made its turn to travel back into the city center. There was a space only a few yards around the corner. Rae slid the Z4 to the curb.

I kept my eyes on the street. Once the FBI agents arrived they'd take over and my part in the case would end.

Strange: Investigations like this were stressful and sometimes frightening. But when one ended, particularly if it slipped into the hands of higher authorities, it left a void that nothing could fill. Gone were the adrenaline highs, the feeling of being on an important mission, the sense of walking on the edge. You were just you again, coping with paperwork and bossing employees and, at home, doing the laundry and taking out the garbage.

Of course, how much excitement can you handle before your adrenal glands wear out? Somebody should do a study.

Something dinged, and I started.

"My watch," Rae said. "An alarm, because I promised Ricky I wouldn't work past midnight, whether he's home or not. He worries about me when I'm on deadline."

Midnight?

It had been a lot more than ten minutes since I'd talked with Baron. Where were the federal reinforcements?

FRIDAY, FEBRUARY 13

SHARON McCONE

I said to Rae, "You don't suppose they got lost?"

She shrugged, the little muscles around her mouth tightening.

"Or are they linked with TRIAD and Verke too?"

"You don't know what to believe anymore. I mean, all those years of lies and cover-ups. Didn't you say the current administration and Congress aren't aware of this organization? Who knows how far their reach spreads? Or what they might do?"

"Then it's best to get out of the car. The feds know exactly where we are."

"And then what?"

"Take the offensive."

"Against the FBI—or whoever you spoke to? Are you insane?"

"Just get out of the car. You don't have to come with me, but you need to be someplace safe."

"The hell I do. I'm in this with you, all the way."

That's my Rae.

We left the car and went east on Taraval, then turned on Forty-seventh Avenue, the street that paralleled La Playa.

This *was* insane, I told myself. Crazy, cracked, berserk, a *folie à deux*. The words that flowed through my mind could have filled an entire page of *Roget's Thesaurus*.

Rae stopped, touched my arm. "An alley," she whispered. "Let's try it."

We inched along past garbage bins, a rusted washing machine, and other detritus. Mud sucked at our feet, and we blundered into ankle-deep puddles. Wind whistled between the buildings, its briny smell reminding me of the surreal journey on San Pablo Bay last night. The alley ended in a high fence. We retreated, walked farther along Forty-seventh, and tried another.

The usual bad smells and stagnant air. I skirted something that looked like a car battery. An animal skittered past us—rat, I thought. Rae nudged me and pointed forward. Another alley lay between the two rows of houses and connected to this one.

We turned down it, and I became aware of the soft crunch of our shoes on gravel. Then a dog in a nearby yard began barking and pulling at its chain.

A window opened and a voice shouted, "Shut up, Attila!"

The dog complied.

Jesus Christ, the brute couldn't be better named.

I spotted Verke's place a few yards ahead, pointed it out to Rae. She nodded and moved forward with me.

The property was surrounded by a high fence like the ones to either side. I looked around. The fence on the property to our left was in disrepair. I went over there, found a gap, and motioned to Rae.

We squeezed through, into a clump of rosebushes. "Shit!" I whispered as thorns pierced my hands.

From here we had a better view of Verke's house. Blinds were closed on all the rear windows except for one, where it and the glass were raised about a foot.

Keeping my eye on the house next door, which appeared to be vacant, I moved along the fence line. Found another loose board and squeezed through. Rae followed. The open window was about ten feet away. Crouching, we approached it.

I saw movement inside as we eased up to the window, Rae on one side and me on the other. I bent down to peer over the sill.

J. T. Verke was a few feet away, on his knees. Two men lay inert on the floor in front of him. He was going through one man's pockets.

Who were they? Fellow TRIAD operatives, most likely, come to take him to task for bungling an important mission. As Verke's killing of Melinda Knowles had proved, TRIAD tolerated no mistakes that could reveal them and their goals.

Verke must have sensed my presence, because suddenly his head came up and he was looking right at me. Eyes as flat and wintery as an ice-bound lake.

Before I could react, his arm came up fast, and the gun he was holding made a low popping sound. The upper part of the window shattered and glass shards rained down on me. I returned fire twice—no time to aim, trusting to instinct.

One of the rounds was a lucky shot. Verke pitched backward and slid toward the hallway.

I let out a heavy breath, felt Rae's supporting arm around my shoulders. Verke lay motionless. The force of my bullet had knocked the gun from his hand; I saw it some six feet away from him under the overhang of a lower cabinet.

I got slowly to my feet, raised the window, and Rae gave me a boost up and over. Watching Verke's still form, I went to pick up his gun and remove the clip. Then, cautiously, I stepped over to him.

He was alive and conscious, his gray eyes soulless and unblinking as he looked up at me.

The wound was high on the right side of his chest and there was no arterial blood. I checked his pulse—thready, but he would probably live. I'd shot to kill—it's what you do in a situation like that—but I was relieved not to have one more lost life on my conscience. One fewer nightmare.

Rae came up beside me. "FBI's banging on the front door," she said. "Silly feds probably underestimated their arrival time or got lost. I'll let them in."

I looked at Verke, and his icy eyes stared back at me.

You don't care about anything, I thought. Not even this ideology you and the others in TRIAD are supposed to espouse. It's all about the intrigue and your ability to inflict pain. I'd like to know what made you that way, but I've got better concerns in my life.

Men's voices rose from the front of the house. Before they came in, I removed Piper's pendant from my neck and swung it back and forth in front of Verke's face, then dropped it on his heaving chest.

WEDNESDAY, JULY 15

SHARON McCONE

Today Congress began an investigation into rogue intelligence agencies. Apparently there're a lot of them out there, composed of "patriots" cut loose by the current administration or angered by its policies. J. T. Verke will be testifying at the hearings; he spilled his guts to federal prosecutors. The microchip that Ryan Middleton smuggled out of Iraq contained proof of rampant covert assassinations, torture, and incitements to uprisings against foreign governments by quasi- and US-sponsored paramilitary organizations. Unfortunately Middleton's motives were less than altruistic: he had intended to sell the chip to the highest bidder.

I don't plan to watch the televised hearings—too depressing. Besides, I've done my part of the job.

Piper has bounced back with her innate resiliency. She's rented a small house in my neighborhood, has gotten her business back on its feet, and is gradually acquiring new possessions. She and I work out almost daily at a new rehab center that's opened on Church Street, close to our homes.

Adah and Craig are getting married next month. He took her back East to meet his parents, and they loved her. They're coming to the wedding that Barbara and Rupert and Hy and I are cohosting at Touchstone—and I'm to be the matron of honor!

Mick and Alison are still going hot and heavy. Ted's new silk fashion statement has worked out well; I think it may become permanent. Gwen Verke is now the Curleys' foster child. This summer she's helping Chelle rehab the house on Chenery Street. Ricky forgave Rae for our dangerous mission—he always forgives her, no matter how outrageous her behavior—and she delivered her novel only a few days late.

Hy's in Vietnam this week. Don't ask me why.

Me, I'm driving again—in my BMW Z4. Ricky, as usual, bought Rae a new car for her birthday, and she gave me a great price on her old one. My beloved old MG went to a collector who restores vintage cars. Next week I start flying, with Hy along as the requisite instructor. By September I'll have my FAA check ride and my license will be reinstated. And next weekend, we'll be going to the city animal shelter to interview cats.

My family, of course, are all nipping at my heels. Ma is less frantic since Melvin's new round of treatments is working. I've agreed to Hy and me attending a big Labor Day weekend gathering at Charlene and Vic's new spread above Santa Barbara. At least they've promised us the guest house with its own little swimming pool.

Life is . . . well, life. It goes on. And so do I.